half-light

half-light

ten stories

stephen o'donnell

portland, oregon

This is a work of fiction. Any resemblance these characters have to actual persons, living or dead, is entirely coincidental.

© 2023 Stephen O'Donnell

"From the Streetcar" was originally published in *Nailed Magazine*.

Cover art: work in progress, *Autumn into Winter*, pencil and acrylic on panel, 2015

Design: Gigi Little

Printed in the United States

ISBN 979-889121974-8

Stephen O'Donnell
128 SE 79th Avenue
Portland, OR 97215
stephenodonnellartist.com

1 2 3 4 5 6 7 8 9

To those who kept telling me I was a writer when I said I wasn't.

Thursday morning, 9:45   1

Joe and Sam spend the night   2

A ceiling of painted birds   11

The leaves at the top   24

From the streetcar   40

In spring, in winter   57

Exiles   65

Two brothers   71

Drop   82

Miss Maureen   89

Afterword   100

Acknowledgments   102

CROSSING, STARTING DOWN the hill on the busy street, the house on the corner, thick to the sidewalk, has well-made steps set exactly at the corner of the lot. A solid concrete staircase leading five steps up to the narrow, sparse yard. The small house that fills the lot in spite of itself, is dingy white and squat, probably built in the forties or fifties. Cheaply. The clapboard siding is incised by the morning light into long running gray pencil lines. The only color anywhere here is the faded red of the Beware of Dog sign set loose beside the meager front porch. My thought is that there is no dog. Or not one anymore.

Even before I cross the street I hear her. And as I start down the slope past the side of the house, from a small window toward the back of the building, right above the sidewalk, a woman is coughing. Not loud or very rough, but persistently. It's an old lady's cough. The window is a blank rectangle, shadowed by a short length of rain gutter, measured only the width of that small window. So I see nothing beyond that blank, but the coughing comes regularly. I think that there is nothing in that small house but that coughing. Along the top of the window, in the very bright sun, two fat-to-bursting sparrows silently hop and turn along the rain gutter.

Joe and Sam spend the night

JOE LOOKED UP from his drink, his eyes, blue or green, blurry in the dim, brownish light of the bar.

"I just don't know how she could have done that. She was as happy about getting married as I was. I swear she was. And then, what, you just change your mind?"

Joe looked down into his drink, already his fourth since Sam had joined him. Just ice, now, in the low, faceted glass. He motioned the bartender for another.

"I don't know what the fuck I'm going to do. I just can't believe it. I just can't . . ."

Sam didn't know what to say. Felt he shouldn't even be there, listening to this. He should have thought of some excuse not to come down; why had he come down? Why had Joe even messaged him? It's not like they really knew each other, not like he knew Joe's fiancée—now ex-fiancée—at all.

"We were looking at places, she was shopping for her dress. I asked my little bother to be my best man. He cried when I asked him. He fucking cried, man."

They worked in the same building, but not in the same office. Said hello at the elevator. They accidentally had lunch together at the same food cart one day, a coincidence they happened to be there at the same time. And a few months later Joe friended Sam on Facebook. Pretty much all they knew about each other was what was posted there. They seemed to agree on politics, liked a lot of the same music, their "laugh" emojis landed in similar places. Joe had the same pretty girlfriend in almost every picture. Sam was gay, with "no relationship info to show." He certainly never shared on Facebook that his boyfriend of nine years had dumped him last fall, that he'd been blindsided, still pretty much devastated.

"I asked my dad for his mother's wedding ring. Can you believe that? Can you fucking believe that? I was going . . ." Joe took a last gulp and, slurring a bit, asked the bartender for another.

"Hey, buddy, maybe you ought to slow down a bit?" Sam, still nursing only his second, looked over at the clock behind the bar, looked over at the bartender, wondering if he was going to cut Joe off at some point. Sam figured with what he'd been through himself, he ought to be able to say something. Something helpful. But he didn't have anything wise to say about how you get over being dumped.

"It's just . . . it's just . . ." Joe's eyes welled up with tears, and he looked away.

"It's okay. It's okay, man."

"How embarrassing. I'm sorry. God. Fuck." Joe started wiping the tears away, then covered his face with his hands. A muffled sob, then an angry shake of his head. He turned away from Sam, breathed, wiped his nose with a cocktail napkin. He coughed, took a moment to breathe, and turned back to Sam.

"Hey. Hey, it was really cool that you came down, man. Why'd you do that? That was really cool." He wiped his eyes with the palms of his hands, smearing his tears back along his temples. "I guess I told you more than you ever wanted to know, right? Hey, now, come on, you tell me how you're doing. What've you been up to?"

"Next time, okay? Getting pretty late. Maybe we ought to call it a night?"

"Yeah, yeah, you're totally correct, sir," shaking his head no, before he slowly nodded yes and smiled.

Joe signaled the waiter to settle the tab, gestured to add Sam's drinks. Sam started to protest, but Joe insisted.

"No. Now, you listened to all my shit. Least I can do. You'll catch me next time."

He signed the bill, his signature trailing off onto the counter. Walked a fairly straight line to the door. But when he went to push it open, his hand connected with the door frame instead.

Outside, shifting on his feet, he started to make a bleary goodbye, but Sam cut him off.

"Hey, you better let me call you a cab. Or, what part of town do you live in?"

Joe said he could drive, no problem, then told Sam where he lived anyway. It was way out. But Sam didn't feel good about leaving him on his own.

"Let me take you, buddy. I'll take you, yeah?"

Joe shook his head, "No, come on, it's too far. That's . . . yeah, okay, thanks . . . you're . . ." He didn't finish, just looked down at the sidewalk and dragged his hand across his face.

HEADING OUT OF DOWNTOWN, Joe turned quiet. Suspiciously quiet. Sam got worried and let down Joe's window.

"Hey, you feel okay? You're not going to throw up, are you? Man, please lean your head out the window if you're going to throw up."

"I'm *not* going to throw up," Joe said almost angry. And threw up.

"Oh, shit."

"Oh, shit."

All down the front of him, the edge of the seat, some on the carpet.

Joe groaned, "Oh, I'm sorry, man . . . gross . . . I'm so sorry . . ." and swiped at his mouth with the sleeve of his jacket.

Sam was pissed. In an extravagant gesture considering the car's age, he'd just had it detailed. So it wasn't just the rising smell that made him anxious, but a desire to clean up the mess and protect his investment. The sooner the better.

They were much closer to his place than to Joe's, so Sam said they'd better stop at his apartment; Joe could make a quick pass at his clothes while Sam cleaned up the car. When they got to the apartment, Joe slowly, carefully unfolded himself from the car, clutched his soiled jacket closed and unsteadily followed Sam inside.

"This is so gross . . . I'm so, so sorry, man . . . So gross," he muttered.

Upstairs, in Sam's small apartment, Sam directed Joe to the bathroom, gave him a towel, told him there might be some ginger ale in the refrigerator, grabbed a can of rug cleaner, a sponge, and a roll of paper towels.

LUCKILY, IT TURNED OUT that most of the damage Joe had done was to himself. When Sam came back upstairs, he found Joe's shirt and pants and jacket hanging awkwardly, dripping wet, wrinkled and twisted, over the back of a chair. In the overlit bathroom, water was splashed lavishly everywhere, the floor almost a pool. The towel was a wet heap in the corner and Joe's wadded up t-shirt was lying, soaked all through, under the sink. A toothpaste tube was open on the edge of the tub.

And Joe, in his boxers and socks, his wet socks, was sitting on the lid of the toilet seat, his head in his hands.

Sam went to put the cap on the toothpaste.

"I didn't use your toothbrush," Joe said, squinting from the light, and looked like he was going to start crying again.

"You minty fresh, now?"

Joe gave a pained "I hope so" and struggled to get up. He was hard, poking through the fly of his boxers. But when he noticed Sam's surprised look, he looked down, said, "Oh, shit!" and fumbled to pull the fly closed around himself.

"Sorry! Sorry . . . so much for whisky dick, I guess," he laughed, his eyes unfocused. But his smile faded quick and he put his head down.

Sam tried to get past the awkward moment by going into the kitchen to get Joe some water. "I'm going to get you some water," he said over his shoulder.

Joe shuffled out of the bathroom, sat down, sitting on the same chair as his wet clothes, and leaned his elbows on the table, rubbing the back of his neck. Sam handed him a glass of water.

"Dude, you're a mess. Your clothes are all wet; you got a bit too carried away with all that. Maybe you . . . maybe you should just stay here. I got extra blankets, you can sleep on the floor. Your clothes should be dry enough in the morning and I can drive you back to your car."

His head propped in his palm, Joe rubbed the cool glass across his forehead. "Sorry to be such a pain in the ass, man. I'm such a fucking idiot! Yeah, just give me a blanket and I'll go to sleep and stop bothering you. Thanks. You're being very cool. Very cool."

When Sam got him the blanket, he immediately wrapped it around himself, shuffled across the carpeted floor, right up to the shaggy throw rug that was beside Sam's low, frameless bed, flopped down on his stomach and pulled the blanket up over his head, his feet, his droopy, wet socks sticking out.

That wasn't really where Sam had in mind for him to sleep. "Uh, are you really going to be comfortable there, right there?"

"Yeah. Yeah, this is great," was the muffled response.

"Need a pillow?"

A barely audible, "No, I'm fine."

"Okay, buddy, you better get some rest. You're going to feel like shit tomorrow, you know."

A moaned, "Yeah . . ."

So Sam mopped up the bathroom, hung the towel, wrung out Joe's t-shirt, smoothed out his shirt and pants, his jacket. He got ready for bed himself and then, with Joe where he was and the bed cornered into the window like it was, he had to crawl over the end of the low bed to get into it. He set the alarm for early enough that he could get Joe to his car and then still get to work on time.

It had been almost a year since he'd slept in the same room with another person, almost a year since David left him. It had taken almost all that time to get used to the absence, the silence, a silence unsettled now by the sound of Joe's breathing. He lay there listening, trying not to, for a long time before he was finally able to get to sleep.

IT WAS MAYBE a few hours later, the dark just starting to fade, that the sounds Joe was making woke him up. He couldn't tell what it was, if he was snoring, talking in his sleep, or maybe crying again. Sam was lying on his stomach, on the side of the bed away from the window, the same side he slept on when David was still on the other side, and he reached down and patted Joe on the shoulder.

"Hey, buddy, you okay?"

"What?" Joe whispered, barely audible.

"You okay?" Sam's hand still on Joe's shoulder.

"I . . . what?" Joe whispered again, rolling part way over but still turned away, reaching up, taking hold of Sam's arm.

"I was just seeing if you were okay," Sam whispered back, wondering at the heat of Joe's hand clutching his arm.

There was a long silent moment before Joe softly muttered, "Hey," and rolled onto his back, not letting go Sam's arm, not turning his face toward Sam. Another moment and he reached his other hand to Sam's arm. Then with both hands, he pulled it closer, pressed Sam's forearm against his cheek. Sam felt the stubble of a man's cheek, the warmth of a man's skin, and through his confusion at Joe's gesture came the ache of what he'd lost when David had packed his things and left.

Sam didn't pull away, and after another long and empty pause, Joe whispered, "Hey, are you awake?"

More silence, Sam not knowing how to answer, until he started, "I . . ."

"Are you awake?" Joe whispered again, so softly, and in another moment gently drew Sam's arm down, leading Sam's hand down till it was on his crotch, where Joe was hard again.

"No whisky."

And he wrapped both of his arms around Sam's arm, moved slowly against Sam's hand until Sam, not thinking now, not trying to understand, eased himself down onto the floor, drew back the blanket and took Joe in his mouth, into his mouth until he came.

After, Sam pulled Joe up into the bed to sleep with him. The two lay flat on their backs, shoulder to shoulder and Joe, shaking a little, slowly slipped his hand across under the covers and put his hand on Sam, as hard now as he had been.

"Should I? Do you want me to?"

"Yeah, if you want to," said Sam.

Joe pulled down the covers and took Sam in his mouth, but after a few seconds he stopped, turned away, and started to cry. "I'm sorry . . . I'm . . ."

"It's okay." Sam drew Joe up beside him. Joe curved his head into Sam's shoulder, his arm around Sam's chest, holding onto him, and cried.

"I'm sorry, I just . . . I just don't know what I'm going to do now . . ."

"Just go to sleep, okay? You should just go to sleep." Sam stroked Joe's hair. "Just go to sleep now."

It had started to rain outside. Only very softly. And Sam was awake once more just as the morning was coming into gray and he wasn't completely sure that he'd ever even been asleep. He looked out the window at the rain now, watched the slow lightening of the sky, Joe in his arms, listening to Joe's breathing, feeling the motion of his breathing. And he held on through this strange and intimate moment, lying there with another person, someone sleeping in his arms, and yet still completely alone.

But he didn't know, couldn't tell from the way they were wrapped together, that Joe was also awake looking out at the rain, the slowly brightening gray. Lying there, they both had the same thought, the same determination, not imagining the other could have it, too: I'll see how long he holds on, I won't let go, won't move away until he does. Lying to themselves that it was nothing more than some sort of early morning good manners, not wanting to wake the other. Lying to themselves that they weren't really both just clinging to each other, both of them lost. But now in this awkward union, this brief and unnatural embrace, the two strangers could hold that loss suspended. So they both waited in this moment, and only Sam knew when the alarm would go.

A ceiling of painted birds

AN OLD POOL HOUSE, a small, domed building built at the farthest extreme of one of those once-glamorous old Long Island estates. The property, each year shabbier, more weather beaten, ran all the way down to the beach. Fenced and hedged off all around. But one morning before dawn Mika, having slept nearby on the beach, and looking for a better, warmer place to stay, to hide out, had found a way in through a gap in the fence.

The girl had been crashing there for more than two weeks, now. The pool house had been the first shelter she'd come to. Half swallowed up by the hedge, with long tendrils of ivy eating into its peeling, sun-bleached paint, it was entirely fronted by several pairs of French doors, their glass panes almost opaque with grime. It faced the long rectangle of an empty, dirty pool. And just beyond that, a low stone wall—its wrought-iron gate forever rusted open—that led through onto a long, broad swathe of lawn sloping upwards to a wide terrace. The main house, vague in the morning gray, rose up there, far off at the other end of the estate.

A locked door handle had broken without much effort. Inside, Mika found a large high-ceilinged room, its ceiling painted with pink birds against a blue-green sky, faded and stained, from which hung a small gilt and crystal chandelier, tangled with cobwebs. On either side were two smaller rooms, a bathroom and a dressing room, proof of the building's former purpose, its purpose now being storage space, filled with what looked to be mostly junk.

Rotting deck chairs, broken flowerpots, as well as scuffed and broken furniture that must have been brought down from the house long ago and forgotten. An over-stuffed armchair with its silk damask split, shredded. A massive pair of baroque and dented brass vases, gone to mottled green. Stacks of sagging cardboard boxes. Shadeless lamps. There were the remains of a Persian carpet on the floor and, on top of a drawer-less chest of drawers, pushed into a corner, the large rounded shape of an ancient Victrola's bell loomed, draped over with a heavy-fringed velvet cloth.

All these things gray with dust.

She'd pulled the cloth down from the Victrola that dawn, wrapped herself in it, and curled up on the floor, her backpack for a pillow, the dust settling around her.

The pool house had been a very lucky place to land. The sink dripped loudly, no hot water, but the bathroom was otherwise functional. The electricity was still connected; she could charge her old iPod. So in the deepest part of night, when she felt most safe, the only sound the muffled sighing of the ocean nearby, she could put her earbuds in, take a few hits of a joint, and almost enjoy her meal of yet another convenience store burrito And after almost three weeks, now, Mika hadn't seen anyone at all except, one afternoon, a man mowing the grass of that vast lawn. Mika had hidden in the dressing room, then, because the door locked from the inside, and she hoped that would keep her safe.

But she didn't know that for those almost three weeks, for nearly all of those almost three weeks of nights, if she lit a joint, the faint, brief flame of it was seen from a bedroom window at the grand, fading house on the terrace at the end of the garden.

THE LAND HAD BEEN BOUGHT, the house built, before the First World War. The Nordens had been one of those rich families like the Vanderbilts and Astors, but their wealth and position, newly won, had dwindled slowly and then fast.

At fifty-nine, Alice Norden was the last of them.

She'd been very shy and quiet as a girl. Her shyness read as aloofness, her quiet as distain. As a young woman, still shy and quiet, not pretty, she was subtly snubbed by others of her social level. She was intelligent and sensitive enough to realize her awkward place in this society, to be embarrassed by the scent of failure and decline that surrounded her family. But also proud and stubborn, she contrived a dignified blindness to the truth.

Both of her parents were gone, divorced and then dead, decades before. And as the years spooled out, she'd stepped back more and more from personal connections. Away from the vague pretense of a social life, away from the disappointment of other people, her life had gradually narrowed, unconsciously but purposefully, until the walls of her house, her property, came to mark the limits of her world. A closed world that seemed to her something like safety, something finally almost comfortable.

There remained her trust fund. Sufficient enough to live on, to pay the taxes on the property. But nothing like enough to slow its encroaching decay. She could have sold the place, certainly; the land alone was worth many millions. But then she would have to leave. And she couldn't leave this house.

She'd long since set the parameters of her existence to include only the sparest essentials, the most limited human contact. For more than a decade, she hadn't been shopping or to a restaurant, hadn't seen a doctor or a dentist. She did her own cooking now, had her groceries delivered to the house, left at the side door. A married couple, Berta and Eduardo, came just twice a month, and then she interacted with them as little as possible. Berta did the cleaning and the laundry, Eduardo mowed the lawn and kept the garden from complete ruin, though Alice almost never went out into the garden anymore.

EVER SINCE MIKA TURNED FOURTEEN, her stepfather had been commenting on her changing body, making jokes about how she didn't look like a little kid anymore. "You're getting some real nice curves, baby girl." He laughed.

Her mom laughed, too, half listening over the sound of the TV. "Hey, but she a good girl, aren't you, Mika, honey? Gotta watch out for them boys . . ." she slurred, reaching for her wine glass without unlocking her gaze from the TV.

Her stepfather didn't work, was around the apartment all the time. And over the next two years, the comments, the jokes, kept coming. There were too many mornings when he barged into the bathroom, knowing she was showering before school. "Oh, sorry!" he'd laughed.

And one night when she was asleep, she woke to the smell of alcohol and her stepfather pulling back her covers.

"What are you doing?!"

She'd jerked the covers away from him, jackknifed her knees up into her chest, turned toward the wall. "Get out of here!" she whispered hoarsely.

"Oh, don't be like that . . . okay, okay . . . I wasn't doing nothing, baby girl. Hey, yeah, but you better go to sleep now . . . you got school . . ."

The last time, two weeks later, drunk again, the smell of it on him, he came into her room while she was sleeping and she woke as he shoved his hand down her pajama bottoms, grabbing between her legs.

She tore away from him, kicking, slapping his shoulder, his chest, his neck. Furious, scared. He laughed, then turned and stumbled out of the room.

Late next morning, with her mom still passed out on the couch in front of the TV, her stepfather having just left the apartment to go down to the corner market for cigarettes, she stuffed her backpack with some clothes, her iPod, and anything else that seemed important in that frantic moment, and snuck into her mom and stepfather's bedroom. She took a gold chain and a ring of her mother's, a bag of pot she found, and zipped it into her backpack. She knew where they kept their tiny bit of emergency cash, and she stuffed the less-than-three-hundred dollars in her pocket and left.

She knew that when she didn't show up for school, when she didn't come home, eventually—eventually—someone would notice. So she'd taken the train down to the beach, trying to get far enough away, someplace where they wouldn't think to find her. After only two nights trying to sleep on the beach—the cold, the beating and hiss of the waves—she'd found that break in the fence.

IT WAS CLOSE TO SUMMER, now, and the heat gathered in the pool house during the sunny days, lingered through the night. Mika would sometimes roll back the rug, then, and lie on the cool tile floor in just a t-shirt and briefs. The nights were short and she'd sleep heavily, sometimes until the middle of the morning, the day already warming.

So she didn't know that Alice, who never slept much, couldn't sleep much, who was always up before the first light, came down through the garden each morning before dawn. In her nightgown and flip-flops, she'd walk close against the hedges and planting beds, skirting the lawn, and curve carefully clear of the massive, long-empty urns that flanked the swimming pool. In the slowly brightening gray, she'd put her hand to a dirty glass windowpane of one of the French doors, to make a shadow so she could see inside, and watch the girl sleeping there.

ONE MORNING, still half dark, Mika woke, pulling herself away from a bad dream. She rolled over and squinted toward the light, saw a shadow there, a shadow that backed away from the glass, turned and started to walk away.

Mika froze, holding her breath.

Even though she was quickly realizing through her confusion that it was too late, that she'd been found out, Mika got up carefully—noiselessly—and tiptoed toward the expanse of cloudy glass, the faint receding figure of the woman beyond. The girl leaned her forehead up against one of the doorframes, then opened the door just wide enough to put her head out.

"Excuse me—" she started, almost a whisper, but her throat was dry and the words came out thick and cracked, inaudible. She cleared her throat and tried again, barely any louder.

"Oh . . . excuse me . . ."

But the woman in the nightgown and flip-flops didn't respond, didn't seem to even hear, didn't stop until, at the far end of the pool, she turned halfway around.

"You know this is private property, don't you."

Her expression was blank, her affect flat. She turned again, turned back toward the house, while Mika stood, clutching the doorframe, not able to let go of the instinct to hide, and watched the woman walk away.

MIKA STAYED AWAY for two days, not knowing what the woman's reaction had been to finding her there, if she'd called the police. She slept on the beach, like she'd done when she'd first run away. She found a better spot this time, more sheltered, a space tucked under a private stairway down to the beach. But it was so cold in the last hours of the night, impossible to sleep, and she returned to the pool house late on the third night.

The lock on the door hadn't been repaired, nothing had been moved inside. Nothing seemed at all different. Mika made a place to sleep for herself farther back from the row of French doors, better hidden, she thought. She covered herself with the heavy velvet cloth and tried to keep herself awake. To see what might happen, if the woman or someone else, a guard, the police, might appear. But warm, finally, she eventually drifted off.

She woke to a faint grating on the window glass. Again, the shadow of the woman against the scant light of dawn.

Mika jumped up, wrapped the cloth around herself,

opened the door part way, but the woman was already walking away.

"You came back," Alice said flatly, without turning around, still walking.

"I'm sorry, I—"

"You can stay there." Alice was well beyond the pool now. Barely audible, she muttered, "I don't care."

THE NEXT MORNING ALICE was there again, but Mika was already awake. When Alice approached one of the windowed doors, the side of her hand against the glass, making shade against the light, Mika went up on one elbow.

Alice quickly stepped away.

Mika scrambled up and gently opened the same door, stood half in, half out of the doorway.

"Please wait," she said softly, the second word almost whispered.

Alice stopped this time, turned and looked at Mika, the same blank look on her face as before. "What are you doing here?"

"I—you said I could stay here. Just yesterday you said so.

"Did I? I—"

For a moment, something seemed to clear in Alice's gaze. Then she turned once more, moving toward the house. But only a few steps more and she stopped beside the dirty, empty pool, looked down into it, searching. She turned back to Mika with that same searching look, then walked away in the lifting gray, her pale nightgown against the long vertical of the dark green lawn.

WHEN ALICE REACHED THE HOUSE, she wrote a note to Berta to tell Eduardo to clean and fill the pool. Only that. "Don't do anything else." She left it where she thought Berta would find it, because she wasn't sure she'd otherwise remember to tell her. She looked down at the disconnected, jagged scribble of her handwriting and hoped Berta would be able to read it.

MIKA WOKE TO THE SOUND of the leaf blower. She quickly crept out of sight, but through a crack in the dressing room door, she watched the gardener clean out and slowly fill the pool, wondering why he was doing it. When Eduardo was done, when she was sure he was gone for the day, she opened one of the French doors part way, sat on the floor just inside, and stared out at the pool, so changed, the sun glancing sharply off the water. Her gaze also ran the length of the long green lawn, up toward the terrace and the big house where the woman lived.

She went down to the beach in the afternoon, but when she came back that night she found a pillow, sheets, and a blanket and a towel in a neat pile in the pool house.

WHEN SHE WOKE the next day, later than usual, Mika turned over and saw Alice standing at the far end of the pool. Only standing there, facing the pool house. Mika didn't start to get up, didn't move, but lay there watching her for a long while, her head on the pillow that Alice had brought, covered with the sheet Alice had brought, before the woman turned and walked slowly back to the house.

Late in the afternoon, almost twilight, Mika ventured beyond the pool, the low stone wall that bordered it, through the rusted-open gate, and farther into the garden than she'd allowed herself before.

The long, gently sloping stretch of lawn that led up to the house was bordered on each side by a row of small walled gardens, each designed on a different pattern, each centered on a different feature—crumbling statuary, dry and long silent fountains, topiary gone shapeless and brown—but all linked and grown over by vines. With each corner that she rounded Mika was met with sad and fascinating decay.

"Did you swim yet?"

Mika, startled, leaned around the edge of a stone wall to find the voice. Alice was standing there, the reflected green of the lawn covering her, submerging her, so that she almost disappeared into the shrubbery against which she stood. When Mika caught her gaze, she turned away, looked off across the lawn. "It was always so nice in the summer."

"Well, I—"

"Grandmother always had little parties for the children down there," Alice said, still not looking at the girl.

"Is that why you had the pool filled? Are you—do you need me—"

Alice turned away, slowly stepped from the shade into the retreating sunlight, "You should at least take a swim. I'm sure it's lovely in this heat."

Mika watched Alice walk away toward the house, neither of them saying anything more. Mika turned and walked away, then, too, returned to the pool house, crossing the open lawn, unhidden.

IT WAS GETTING DARKER. Mika had never dared to turn on any lights at night. But now, not knowing if it even worked, she pushed the switch to the chandelier. More than half the lights still lit, and an amber wash settled along the dust and shadows of the junk-filled room. Feeling even bolder, she unlocked, unlatched the row of French doors, opened all of them wide—only one resisted, stuck shut—the clean, warm air washing into the long-closed-up room.

She sat in the doorway, then, cross-legged, lit a joint, not bothering to hide that either. She sat, looking at the soft ripples on the pool's surface, the color of the water's reflections changing as the sky turned away from blue to gray to gold to orange to gray again, the sun already lost down behind the trees now. The evening was still, and the smoke Mika exhaled drifted lazily toward the water, descending, dispersed.

Mika stood up, took off her shoes and her jeans, walked to the edge of the pool, the shallow end, put her toes in. It was still very warm from the long day of sun. The pool had no steps that led down into the water, so she sat, swung her hips out over the edge and dropped herself in, the water reaching up to her waist. She leaned forward until all of her, her face and hair, was wet, and swam forward into the deep end.

She swam back and forth, the splash and ripple of the water the only sound that night, even the ocean so close seemed to have gone quiet. She dived down where the water was deepest, coming up again and again, looking up through the water to the lights of the chandelier, that seemed to float somehow in the quickly deepening dark.

Coming up from the bottom again, she opened her eyes, looking for the lights, but this time a bright shape came alongside. Mika's face broke the surface, she wiped the water from her face, and saw that it was Alice striding confidently toward the pool house. She wasn't wearing a nightgown this time, but a long, loose white linen dress, a flat, square mass of something held to her chest.

Without looking down toward Mika as she passed, "I found my grandmother's old 78s. I'd forgotten the Victrola was down here."

She stepped into the pool house and over to the corner of the room where the Victrola was, bent down and let the records spill out from her arms onto the carpet. Lying scattered at her feet were recordings by Russ Columbo, Paul Whiteman, Ruth Etting, Rudy Vallée. She picked one up and held it out into the dim light of the chandelier.

"Oh, this one." Her voice rose into the domed ceiling of the room, the ceiling with its painted birds, "Grandmother always played this. I guess it's a waltz."

Alice wound the crank of the Victrola, took the heavy shellac disc out of its sleeve and placed it onto the turntable, then swung the brake lever forward, watched the record set to turning, and dropped the needle down.

A few seconds of scraping and static that echoed across the ceiling and out into the night, and then the sound of clock chimes striking three o'clock and, after a beat, the lilt of Whiteman's band came through.

Alice continued to stare down at the spinning 78, but then she turned her profile to the rows of open doors, smiled, tilted her head back. "Do you hear that? Isn't it funny, so old-fashioned. Yes, that's a waltz." Turning her face toward Mika, she looked past the girl and out into the night. "You've probably never even heard a waltz," and she smiled to herself again.

Mika was in the shallow end, crouched down, only her head and shoulders rising above the surface of the water. She listened to the scratchy record, the music that seemed so fragile and odd, not knowing what to think, trying to find something to say, her mouth open with words that wouldn't come.

Alice looked down at her, now, didn't turn away, finally seemed willing to try, maybe, to search for some sort of a connection with this stranger.

Mika, still confused and wordless, embarrassed by the woman's direct gaze, had to look away. She shivered.

Alice stepped forward to the edge of the pool.

"Are you ready to come out? Here, let me help you."

"I'll get you all wet."

"Don't worry. Here."

Alice reached down, clasped Mika's arm, the t-shirt's dripping sleeve stretching under the woman's grasp, and the girl reached up and took hold, too, the wet of her fingers spreading into the white linen sleeve.

The leaves at the top

WAY UP, THE GRAY green leaves against the gray green sky, almost the same color, almost no color. But in the warm, dry breeze the long curved leaves turned, rose and fell and twisted, flashing bright silver in the muted afternoon light.

Beneath the tall bulk of a eucalyptus tree, the girl lay on the low slope, just down the embankment from the long, straight road. Stretched out on a mess of discarded leaves, long, narrow strips of bark and the small metal-colored tree berries, her feet and her worn-to-nothing kicked-off shoes sprawled into the fat line of bright green grass growing along the irrigation ditch that ran straight along down the hill from the road.

She squinted up at the tree, the like of which she'd never seen. Inhaled the gray green smell of it. Seemed so clean to her, the cleanest thing she'd ever smelled. She lay there watching the leaves turning way up high, at the top, leaves flashing like silver spangles.

It was her latest ride that put her there, under that tree. She was always careful, calculating about hitching a ride from a boy or a man who was driving alone, but it'd been so hot, right in the hottest part of the day, when he stopped and asked. And he said he was headed all the way to Fresno, right where she wanted to go. He looked to be only a few years older than she was, probably just out of high school. He had glasses and too much hair grease. Scrawny and nervous and had a cough. She figured, tough farm girl that she was, she could always take him if she needed to.

They hadn't driven very far, and by the road signs she figured they were still about ten miles south of Fresno, out in the middle of nowhere, when he wheezed and coughed and pulled the Tin Lizzie sharp off the road, parked under that tall eucalyptus tree. He told the girl to get out of the car. She said no, asked him what he was stopping for. He didn't answer her, just coughed again, his face bright red now. He reached back, grabbed her twine-bound, crumbling cardboard valise and threw it out of the car.

"What the hell you doin'?!" she yelled.

The valise had landed hard, slid down the shaded embankment, and she scrambled out of the car, stumbled down from the road after it.

But when she turned back the boy was right in front of her, his glasses flashing crazy in the bright sun. He shoved her down on the loose layer of eucalyptus leaves. Started to come down on her. She kicked her leg into his knee, swung both arms across his shoulder hard. Sent him rolling away from her down the slope.

He wrestled himself right, sitting up into the rising dust, rubbing his knee and moaning, hissing with the pain. His red face, his glasses flashing, he wheezed and coughed again. And started to cry.

Raised up on her elbows, she just stared at him for a few moments, then started to laugh. Huffing with anger now, the boy, smearing his tears across his red face, struggled up and came toward her again. She sat up quick, her fists up quick. He stopped, breathing hard. Then with a grinding noise in his throat, he turned and scrambled up the bank, into the car, slamming the door.

The car wouldn't start up. The motor choked and squawked, and she started laughing again.

"That car of yours sounds even worse than you do!"

He jerked his head around. "Stupid bitch!" But his voice pitched too high, and she laughed even harder.

The car finally started, the boy gunned the engine and skidded away, dust and grit billowing down onto the girl from the road. She waved it away from her face, shook it out of her hair, still laughing, and lay back down where she was. No scrawny kid was going to get anything from her, not for nothing, anyway.

The first time, when she was only eight, was gotten for free. Her uncle Hank, her mama's halfwit baby brother. She didn't know what he was trying to do, didn't know to try and stop him. Then it only hurt a little, because he couldn't really do it. Then he cried, too.

When she was twelve, she did it with Cal Jenkins back out behind his grandpa's chicken coop. She didn't mind it so much. She liked Cal and thought he was a fine boy. She didn't like when his friends Joe Borden and Vernon Shanks did it, though. Did it because Cal said she should let them. That same year, though, the year she started looking more like a woman, having more of a woman's body, she also came into the muscle that came with having to do more work on the farm. From then on, she wouldn't let a boy do it unless she let him, unless she wanted to or got something out of it.

When she was fourteen, in the spring, she figured she'd made a mistake and was going to have a baby. She was mad. She knew better, she was a farm girl. So she was glad that by the summer, before anyone had noticed, it bled out of her.

A couple of months later, her papa was killed on the road, walking home drunk in the Oklahoma moonlight.

Her mama went to bed and didn't get up for three months. The farm was far enough south to miss the worst of the Dust Bowl, but the Depression did the worst anyway. Even before her papa had been killed, they knew for sure they'd lose the place soon enough. The girl tried to sell whatever she could to get food for herself, for her little brother and sister. But nobody had any money, people were taking what they could salvage, what they could carry, and heading west. Then the farm was foreclosed, and when the state came for her brother and sister; she lied and said she was already sixteen and could fend for herself, that her mama needed her to work. Two weeks later, the night before the land agent came to run them off, she found her mama hanging in the empty barn.

She didn't have the money for a proper burial, but she let Mr. Aylward, the funeral man, do what he wanted with her, so he'd bury the woman proper enough.

Next morning, she took what clothes she had that were decent, what clothes of her mama's that were decent, put them in that cardboard valise, and started walking toward California.

Lying there in the shade of the tree, she laughed again thinking of that stupid boy who'd left her there. Figured he was pretty desperate to try and do that thing, the thing that boys have to do, that they have to prove, that he was picking up strangers off the road. In the two weeks she'd been on the road, most of the people who'd helped her out had been good enough folk, offering what they had. Which was pretty much nothing, all anyone had these days, anyone on the road. She stayed clear of the camps, afraid to rest, afraid to get slowed down by other people. She was mostly able to catch rides in the backs of trucks that somehow had room for one more, and she was glad enough to help watch out for the children she rode with, letting the mothers of babies get a little sleep. Everyone was so tired, seemed like the whole world was tired.

There were men, too, men by themselves, who sometimes gave her rides. Men who gave her some money when they were done with her. One middle-aged man, bald and pale, said he couldn't pay her after he'd said he would, after he'd done what she said he could. Said he'd lied about having it. She hauled off and bloodied his nose, before she grabbed her valise and slammed the car door behind her. He was so shocked, her standing at the side of the road cussing him up and down, that he just sat there, the motor running, blood running into his wide-open mouth, before he slammed the car into gear and tore off.

Since she was eight years old—almost half her life—she had been learning what men were, what they wanted. And what they didn't care about. Who they never cared about. They didn't care, so neither did she. She wasn't afraid of men. And that's why she could laugh if off that way. Laugh that some boy would think that she would be too afraid, too dumb, that she would let him do it to her. Do it for nothing. That's why she could lie there after that. Lie there in the shade of a huge eucalyptus tree, in the warm of a fine

California afternoon. She could breathe in the strange gray green smell of the tree, look up into the highest branches, the turning gray green leaves that disappeared into the color of the sky. And let herself think of nothing.

THEY LIED TO ME about Fresno. Ain't really no better than where I come from. And they sure lied about bein' jobs there, 'cause they weren't none. Not for no Okies, anyhow. And, oh, folks sure as hell made it plain you wasn't wanted there, hated the sight of you, all but spit at you in the street. But I didn't know none of that that first night.

I had just about enough money left on me for one night's sleep at some mean hotel. I figured I could get me a room, get myself cleaned up, pin up my hair and, next morning, put on my best clothes and look respectable enough that someone maybe give me a job. When I did find me a cheap place to stay, the old lady behind the desk looked me right up and down, stared at me over her glasses.

"You gotta pay in advance. And you're out in the morning. I know how you Okies are and I just don't put up with your nonsense. You can't pay, you can't stay. You understand me, girl?"

I said, "Yes, ma'am," knowing I'd be out the next morning for sure. The room weren't much, but it was a far sight better than the side of the road. And, oh my, when I gone down the hall to wash up, how did that bath feel! I ain't never had a bath in a real tub like that before, with hot water out of the tap and all. We just had us an old tin wash tub at home.

I slept good that night. Sure I did. Next morning, that old lady was beating on my door before I'd even got the pins all out of my hair. Saying I gotta pay up for the next night or get out. I told her I'd be goin', but could I just leave my valise somewheres there? Told her I gotta go look for a job, and it don't look right me carrying it round with me. I asked it real nice. She shook her head, grunted something under her breath, but let me.

I walked up and down every street of that goddamn town, I swear I did. Walked into every store and shop. Got looked up and down, got the back of every goddamn boss turned on me before I could even say a word. Always "No place for you, girl!" Everybody'd said it was gonna be better in California, that people was friendly. But every- where I went, every cold-hearted citizen looked at me like I was just another damn dirty Okie stinkin' up their town.

Except the boys. Except the men in the street, and the men who wouldn't even think about givin' me any kind of decent job. I reckon you know how they was lookin' at me.

Sun was goin' down. I was hungry and hadn't got no place to sleep. I guess I been a fool to think things'd be better here, but I ain't no fool. So if this whole damn town was tryin' to tell me I was only good for one thing? Well then? Couple hours later I went back to the hotel, paid for another night. When I give her the money, old lady looked at me like I stole it. But she sure took it.

Two whole weeks I tried to get me a decent job, or any damn kind of job. Kept getting shooed out of every place I asked, people callin' me names. And every night I got hungry, and every night I had to pay for my room. So I done what I done.

One night this guy tells me I'm pretty. Says I'm too pretty to be hanging around in dark corners, waiting in alleys. Says I ought to go work up at Ma Jenny's, out past the depot. For a minute I didn't have no idea what he was talking about, but I caught on quick enough.

But I figured, somehow I figured even then, that once you go to work at a house you ain't never got a chance of a regular life after that. Can't go back to your old life, if you got one. Can't go back to your family, if you got any. Just can't lie your way out of it, like what you maybe, maybe didn't do in some alleyway one time or another.

But then after days and days trying to get me a more decent way to keep myself goin', I give up. Think to myself, I gotta eat, ain't I? Think to myself, it's nothin' I ain't done already to get along. So what's so wrong. Least I'll get a roof over my head. So I find my way out there to this Ma Jenny's place, out there past the depot. Middle of the day when I get there. Great big house, nice once, I reckon.

A big ugly guy was hanging round the front door, sitting in a broken chair, smoking, cigarette butts all over. His name is Henry. I told him I want to talk to Ma Jenny. He looks me up and down and says what I gotta talk to her about. I tell him she'll want to talk to me. I just stand there, all tough like. He looked me up and down again and goes inside. When the door opens back up a big woman stands there in her housecoat. Not young, not by a mile. Rouged up. Yellow hair that ain't her own. Sun in her face making her squint, she looks at me hard. Seemed like a long minute she stares at me with her black eyes.

"You come in, girl."

Ma Jenny took me along to her back parlor. She set down in a big leather chair, behind her big desk, all heavy carved wood. She asks if I know who she is. I tell her I sure do. And if I know about this place. I say I sure do.

She made a sort of grunt. "Go on and tell me your story then, girl."

I ain't never told no one all of it till then. But it felt good to tell it, right to tell it. 'Cause I could see that she understood how I was, what I been through. She made something kind of like a smile, something halfways between a groan and a sigh, when I finished tellin'.

"Alright, girl. Alright."

I lied about how old I was when she asked me, and maybe she knowed it. She says am I sure I want to come live there in that place. And I said I did. I weren't really all that sure, and maybe she knowed that, too. She crossed her big arms over her big front and stared at me hard with her black eyes.

"I got a feeling about you, girl. I don't know. But you don't seem stupid like the rest of them girls." She nodded her head real slow. "Just maybe you'll be alright . . ."

She said she got a place for me if I wanted it. Some girl run away. Left with a broke down farmer. Said she done it before, and Ma Jenny said she couldn't come back there no more, even if she begged. She said she got a nice room for me, sunny during the daytime. She gave me all the rules of the house, told me she'd throw me out on my ass—that's what she said—if I didn't follow 'em.

The room was nice like she said. Most of the other girls was nice enough, too, but kind of silly, kind of stupid like she said. Ma Jenny took things slow with me at first, 'cause she knowed what she was doing. How to get a new girl started, especially one so young like me. So she don't get scared off. Not too many men, not too often. So it weren't too hard to get used to.

I kept pretty much to myself. Daytimes, the other girls was always gabbing with each other, smoking, messing with their hair, reading the picture magazines and trying to make themselves up like the movie stars. Most I ever done was put my hair up in pin-curls. Funny how I was always curling up my hair, then it goin' straight again, Ma Jenny always nagging me to fix up my hair. Make myself more feminine. But I didn't cry or make scenes or sneak in booze like some of the other girls done. And I was still really young, brought in good customers, and I never made her any fuss, and I know she liked that. She always told me, "You got sense." And then she'd say right quick, "But fix up your damn hair," and let out a sound something between a sigh and a laugh.

The men that come to the house was mostly from in town. A few of 'em came over all the way from Chowchilla or even Merced, afraid to get their fun too close to home. They'd sit in the front parlor, all pinked up by the pink colored lampshades we had in there. They'd usually behave pretty good. Ma Jenny wouldn't take no nonsense, wouldn't put up with no rowdies or drunks. Ma Jenny was what you might call right formidable. And what with her and big old Henry, nobody never really caused no trouble. The men that came round was mostly somebody's dad or even somebody's granddad. Some of 'em were just lonely old sad sacks. It was only the young ones was tryin' to prove something. And sometimes they proved the wrong thing, if you know what I'm tellin' you.

And Ma Jenny let the Mexicans come, too. Some places don't. But she reckoned that if they got the money and don't cause no trouble, ain't no harm in lettin' 'em come. White folks call 'em "dirty Mexicans," and some of the girls just won't go with 'em. But they ain't dirty. Cleaner than most from what I seen. And they ain't rough. I never had any kind a problem with 'em.

All us girls was careful to fix ourselves up after a man leaves, making sure he didn't leave nothin' behind. Sometimes it don't work, though. Old Doc Aaron came by once a month or so to check on us girls. He weren't supposed to know what's goin' on here, and if he'd ever met any one of us in the street, he woulda said he don't know us. But he made sure we hadn't got nothin', and when one of us got in trouble he done fixed that, too. That's always a bad business, though. I got trouble three, four times, and Doc Aaron got it out of me. Said I might not be able to have babies if I done it too much. Some of the girls'd still talk about getting a fella and having a baby someday, but you can't go dreaming about things like that when you're in a place like this. I told you most of 'em was kind of stupid. Wouldn't see me thinking about fellas and babies.

This Mexican boy, Sal, started coming to see me about two years after I come to the house. I have to say he was about the prettiest boy I ever been with. His big shiny brown eyes, eyelashes like a girl. Skin so soft, the color of car'mel sugar. And he was so shy and sweet with me. And when we done it, I didn't really mind it at all. I guess I liked him better than anyone, might have done it with him even if I ain't been working at the house. Treated me like I was something special, the way he'd take my hand, look me right in the eyes, tell me I was pretty and nice. Nobody said things like that to me, least not the way he did, or looked at me like that.

After we done it, we'd always lay there in the bed and talk a spell. And he'd talk about how he was gonna get rich one day. He'd get this dreaming look, this far-off look in his big brown eyes. He'd stroke my arm and say, "You know, I'm gonna make so much money. You better believe me. I'm gonna buy me my own farm. And I'm gonna send so much money to my momma and my brothers down in Mexico"—he said it May-hee-co—"and build my momma a great big house." He'd go on and on. And I'd say, "Sure you will, honey."

But, hell, I thought, you're just a Mexican. You ain't got any more chance of getting ahead than I do. Only difference between the two of us is that he thought he could do it. A lot of the men jawed on about their lives, what they was gonna do someday. And if any of 'em made it good, I can't really say I gave a damn. But Sal was so sweet, and something got to me when he told me about them pie in the sky dreams of his. Probably 'cause I knowed, for him, there weren't no chance in hell.

More times than once, Ma Jenny came bangin' on the door, told him he had to get out, that he had his time. Then she told me not to get stupid about no men, sure not about no Mexican. Only thing that ever really got her mad at me, me getting friendly with Sal. She woulda been mad, too, if she'd knowed I'd got in trouble around that time, probably from spending time gabbing with Sal instead of cleaning up after we done it. I didn't say nothin'. But I started thinking. Or not thinking, were more like it. 'Cause for once—just once—I let myself be a fool. Starting thinking how maybe he wouldn't mind so much where I been and what I done, that maybe he'd want me and this thing growing in me.

Some girls went away from the house, made a life and never came back. Maybe it weren't too late for me, neither. I don't know if what I had in me was Sal's or any other guy's, but it was something I thought I wanted right then. For just right then I wanted it.

Last time I seen Sal we was laying in bed after, like usual. I remember he was winding a bit of my hair around his finger, kinda sweet, while he was talking all his nonsense about making it big. And then he said another thing, somethin' he ain't never said before. Said, "When I get my money, when I get my place, I'm goin' back home to Mexico and get me a nice, sweet little wife, and we'll have lots of kids, you know."

And I ain't never saw that coming. Kicked me right in the middle. Don't know how I ever let myself be so damn stupid to think anything might be different, that this boy was different. I was just so sick and ashamed when he said that I just about wanted to die.

He said, "I got me a little gal there, already, waitin'." A cousin or something. He looked at me, gave me a big smile, his eyes all wide, like to tell me how pretty she was. He kept talking, but I didn't say nothin'. What could I say? I didn't let on how it made me feel, him laying there next to me, we just done what we done. He just showed me what a fool I been, showed me right there that I wasn't nothin' to him. He just said it, clear as day. I looked into his pretty, girl eyes and he was so happy and feeling so fine and dreaming. And I knowed he didn't see me at all.

Couple days later, before I had to get Doc Aaron to do it, it came out of me, so maybe like he said I couldn't be having no babies.

Time went along, and about five years of me living in the house, Ma Jenny got to slowin' down. I think she was already sick but didn't want to let on. Like she always said, I was the smart one, so she made me to take on some of the things she always watched after. In the next few years, I worked with her more and more. Got so I didn't work much with customers no more.

"Girl, you're gonna look after things when I'm gone. You're the only one who can do it." She always said it and I always just laughed.

But I started bein' the one who made sure stuff got done round the house. Made sure the gals who cooked and cleaned for the house was on to it. Made sure food got bought, and the doctor come like he was suppose to. Eventually, I started takin' care of the money. Made sure all the bills got paid, made sure people who had to get paid off to leave us alone done got paid off. After about eight years, I was pretty much runnin' things around the house.

Ma Jenny died two years ago September. Eat up with the cancer. She spent her last days most all the time sittin' quiet in the dark in her back parlor. Holdin' on. Then, when it got real bad, she passed quick, just like that. It was hard. And the girls didn't know what was gonna happen to them. But I took over the business. Just like Ma Jenny'd said I got to. Not something I coulda ever seen happening. But I think Ma Jenny taught me right. I'm tough with the girls but I'm good to 'em. Give 'em a bit more of the cut than Ma Jenny did. And it seems I got the knack for pickin' the right ones to work here at the house. I ain't really had to put up with much nonsense at all. The bills are paid on time, the place ain't fallin' down, and me and the gentlemen of the police force—that's what I call 'em—get along just fine. No complaints either side.

Only thing, I feel bad I never went and got my brother and sister. Only kin I have in this world. John and little Barbara weren't hardly more than babies when I run off. But things didn't turn out like I planned, did they. Couldn't bring 'em here. Couldn't let on what I was doin' all these years. So I just hope they been brought up good, better than we ever had it. I like to tell myself that they're doin' all right. With everything being how it is, I sure can't go looking for 'em now. And I hope they never come looking for me.

Nothin' much else I got to fret about, though. Business is steady. And I hear we might have another war coming up. I reckon wars is always good for business. Soldiers gotta have it, you know. We'll just see how it goes. For now, though, I tell you things is pretty good. Everything runnin' along just fine. And on most afternoons, before we open, the girls napping, I can just set in the back parlor and be quiet. Things is nice and settled and I can just be quiet for a moment or two and think of nothin'.

SHE MUST HAVE FALLEN asleep for a few minutes, maybe longer. She never slept deeply these days. Too much to watch out for. So she sometimes had trouble knowing if she slept or not. She stretched her arms up over her head. The shade was deeper now and, squinting up at the patches of sun shifting, filtering through the leaves of the tree, she realized it was getting late in the day. She sat up, turning, kicking one of her shoes a bit farther down into the patch of grass. She kneeled her way to the shoe, sat back down, put it on, reached over and put on the other. All the while crushing the tangle of eucalyptus leaves and bark beneath her. That strange smell, cleanest thing she'd ever smelled.

But the sun was getting lower. And Fresno was about another ten miles off. Folks said it was a good place, people were friendly, and there was work. She was fifteen, almost sixteen, and maybe there was still a chance she might get ahead. Make something like a proper life. Maybe go back and get her brother and sister someday.

She stood up, smoothed down the wrinkles in her worn dress. Ran her fingers rough through her hair, then reached down and picked up her beat-up valise. She climbed to the top of the embankment, stood—one foot in the dirt, one on the pavement—and turned toward what she figured was north. Where she was headed was still about ten miles down the road.

From the streetcar

THE BOY STANDS, LEANING into the corner, moving gently with the motion of the streetcar. His curly light brown hair low across his eyebrows, his baggy jacket, his baggy pants, his Vans. One hand rests on the edge of his up-ended skateboard. The tilting in of the board and the turn of his wrist and the set of his hips as he braces against the wall, is accidentally elegant.

He looks and I look away.

He got on at the same stop as I did. Right away, from the other end of the streetcar, I noticed him looking. That back and forth game. Look and he looks away, look again and he looks away. I remember this game from when I was younger. But this boy is fourteen? Fifteen, at most. I'm more than thirty years older than he is, balding, soft in the belly, so it can't be the game. Not with me. He looks and I look away.

I lean against the vibrating door. In the glare of the overcast sky and the streetcar's hard fluorescent light, the other passengers look gray and rounded off, thick in their winter clothes. The rain stopped hours ago, but it's damp and sour in here. And too hot. When the doors slide open at someone else's stop, the sharp air that blows across my face, I pull it in and hold it in my lungs.

When I reach my stop, I keep myself from looking one last time. To see if he'll look away one last time.

I pivot out through the opening streetcar doors, down from the concrete platform, and down the three more blocks toward my apartment. I walk fast. The sidewalks are pasted thick with fallen leaves. The tapping of my shoes, the sharp gray sky. The air is cold in my lungs. And how pathetic I am. How stupid.

I climb the front steps, the rasping of my shoes on the wide concrete treads. My bag is too full and too heavy. I turn the key in the lock, pull open the door to the foyer. I step back with the swing of the door and have that feeling, that pull in the air like someone is standing behind me. I turn and it's the boy.

I can't make sense of the skateboard tucked under his arm, the baggy clothes, the heavy tangle of hair, the dark brown eyes looking at me. I stare at the boy, there on the steps, maybe ten feet away, and have no idea who he is. And, of course, I know exactly who he is. But I can't knit together this moment. Two, three, four seconds.

I turn, walk in quick and up the stairs, the heavy front door closing soft behind me.

IN MY TINY APARTMENT, three flights up, I lean against the door and catch my breath, turning the bolt behind me. The boy on the steps. I take off my gloves, fold them, put them into my left coat pocket. I put my bag and umbrella into the corner where I always leave them. The umbrella slides, then clatters to the floor. I take off my coat, unwind my long scarf. In my mind I see the boy standing there in front of me on the steps, looking at me. And then I turn and leave. I'm home, this is where I live and he doesn't, so

I turn and leave. I hang up my coat, I hang up my scarf. I take off my watch and leave it where it goes, in the dish on the small table.

The apartment building is U-shaped, and I can see the front door from my kitchen window. I go into the kitchen and part the curtains with the back of my hand. He's still there. Just sitting there, his skateboard angled on the steps beside him. But then his face tilts upward into the light, and he turns his head back and forth, searching. I step back, the thin curtain holding to the sleeve of my sweater, arcing out until I shake it free.

It's cold, and I turn on the old electric wall heater. The rows of horizontal coils come on, buzz, and glow bright pink.

I sit at the kitchen table, trying to concentrate on the work I brought home, tapping the thick stack of papers with the dull end of my pen. I go and stand at the window. Hidden by the thin edge of the curtains, rolling the pen between my fingers, I watch him sitting there, the teenage jittering of his feet on the steps.

The sky looks like rain again. The slow whine of a fire engine a few blocks away. I look over at the clock. I sit down, stare at my work, listen to the breathy pull of traffic down below. I go and stand at the window. Two of my neighbors are there in the courtyard talking to the boy. He looks up at them, his face tilts up into the light again. He smiles, then looks down and they go into the building.

I toss my pen onto the table, start to go into the living room, stop and stand in the wide archway that separates the kitchen and the living room. I scan the room, looking for something, I don't know what. I turn around and go back into the kitchen. And there's the pale green of the shopping bag, folded, on top of the refrigerator.

When I push open the big front door, he turns his head. His shoulders lift, his back straightens. It's only a slight movement he makes, but it's like he expands a little, unfolds.

I look away, I look down. I keep going down the steps. "Waiting for someone?"

I pass him on the steps.

"No . . ." His voice is soft, but deeper than I expect.

"Oh." I'm past him now, and there's nothing else to say as I walk away.

MAYBE TWENTY MINUTES LATER, I turn into the court-yard, carrying my bag. Walking the length of that space, I look at the ground, I look up at the windows, I look at the leafless bushes in the planters. Because the boy is still on the steps.

As I get closer to him, he straightens his back, slides his hand over the flat of the skateboard. The scrape of its wheels on the concrete as he pulls it toward him, holds it against his hip.

Not looking at him, looking at his hand, at the soft bend of his wrist. "It's getting kind of cold out here."

His head tilts up and he squints into the dim light. And in that moment I look at the boy and try to calculate the breadth of his shoulders, the bright childish color of his cheeks.

His eyes still scanning the heavy gray sky. "Yeah, a

little bit. Hope it doesn't start raining again." He looks back at me now, his mouth, still a child's mouth, twisting slightly, almost a smile.

I look down again, at his fingers curved over the edge of the skateboard. And then I look just past his eyes, make a carefully vague smile, and continue up the front steps. I pause at the door, but don't turn around.

AN HOUR LATER. An hour and a half. I go and stand at the window. It's night, it's completely dark, and he's still there, sitting in the green glare of the two big standard lamps at either side of the front steps. His arms crossed tight into his chest, shifting on the cold concrete. And his face tilts up again, flashes of green lamplight in his eyes as he looks from dark window to bright window to dark. I take a step back, but he squints away from the hard green light and looks down again. He pulls his skateboard closer.

A thin grit of rain on the window. As I step up into the shadow of the curtain again, it comes faster. Down on the steps the boy grabs his collar, pulling it up, pulling it tight against the back of his neck. He draws his elbows in, and tucks his head down into his knees.

"HEY, KID! You can't sit there. You can't just sit there in the rain."

He turns and looks up at me, his shoulders hunched tight. I stand with the door propped open, the light of the foyer at my back, and he squints hard, searching to find my eyes in the shadow of my face. I wait for him to say something. But he just sits there shivering, the rain heavy, weighting the soaked curls of his hair, dripping off his nose and his chin.

And this is the moment.

"Come here for a second."

He grabs his board and climbs quickly out of the rain, two steps, three. He stops in front of me, green lamplight in the falling, dripping rain behind him, green lamplight in the wet of his hair. A thin wedge of yellow from the ceiling lamp in the foyer lights up half his face, one shoulder, his pale, wet hand gripping the up-ended skateboard. The rest of him is in my shadow. I step to the side, and the yellow light spreads across him. With the palm of his hand, he pushes the dripping hair sideways off his forehead, his chin lifts. There's no smile there, really, just the shine of the rain on his mouth. I can smell his wet hair. His wet clothes.

"What are you doing out here?"

His mouth goes soft and he looks away. And I ask questions that sound so stupid. Where his family is, if he has somewhere to stay tonight. But he doesn't say anything.

The light is full on him but my face is in shadow, so I'm not afraid to look at him now, to look at his dark brown eyes. I watch them focus on my hand, my hand that holds the door open. I watch as they trace the rectangle of the doorframe. I watch when they tense and try to focus on my own eyes, eyes they can't make out because my face is just a shadow. And when they look past me, past my shoulders, into the bright foyer.

The two of us waiting. He shivers, his head tilting back. He looks at me, searching my face again, something of a smile in his eyes. He looks away. He looks like a good kid. There's kindness in his eyes.

And this is the moment.

"Well . . . I guess you can stay here tonight. I guess you could sleep on the couch. You have to go in the morning, though, okay?"

There's a low sound in his throat, and he looks up at me, the same half smile in his eyes. The smallest nod of his head, and some last beads of rain roll down and drip from his hair. I can smell his hair.

UP THREE FLIGHTS, our thudding, scuffing footsteps on the stairs, the creak of the banister, the dampened dust and dirt of the carpet. The whole time going up, with him in back of me, I keep questioning this thing I've done, this opening I've made or let happen, by letting him in. And my thoughts keep running into corners.

In my apartment the light is low, as always, but that seems like an odd thing, now, how dark it is. And it feels awkward locking the door behind us. He leans his skate- board up against the wall in the corner where I always leave my umbrella. I turn the heat up and give him a towel for his wet hair. He takes off his jacket and shoes. Otherwise, he's not that wet. He asks if he can use the bathroom. He doesn't close the door all the way. I don't know what to do then, and I go into the kitchen and fuss and tidy the work papers on the table until I hear the toilet flush.

We're both hungry. Spaghetti is fine with him. He sits on the hard wooden chair at the kitchen table, not saying much, while I cook the pasta. His plain, dark eyes follow me, watching every routine movement I make, as if it were an unusual thing I was doing or somehow strangely graceful.

And I watch him, too, trying to fill my quick, falsely casual glances with as much as I can. I take in how the dim light shining down catches the blond ends of his lashes, the blunt end of his strong nose. I notice, in the shadow of the messy fullness of his hair, the strength of his neck, the still-childish bones arching at the stretched-out collar of his t-shirt. His calm hands. The loose set of his knees. And his big feet, the damp, not very white socks.

I open a bottle of wine, and as I hold the glass up into the dim light and the red wine pours into it, our gaze connects though the thin glass.

"So, how old are you anyway?"

"Not old enough. But I drink wine sometimes."

I pour him half a glass.

He takes a small, cautious sip of the wine, holding the bowl of the glass cupped in his hand. He turns in his chair, tilting his head toward the window, and looks out at the rain, the heavy, slicing threads lit up by the streetlight.

I think about how young he must be. What grade in school he must be in. I think about what I remember about high school. What time has made in my mind of those ugly years of high school. And I try to remember who I was, then. And I wonder how I became the way I am now, how a person gets from one place to the other. And if I'm any different, really, than the boy I was then, if anyone is really any different.

And then I'm looking at his mouth, the stain of red wine on his mouth, and I haven't noticed that he's not looking out the window anymore, but at me. He takes another careful sip of wine. He smiles at me and I look away.

WE EAT OUR DINNER at the little table and talk about movies and graphic novels and new music, none of which I know anything about. I tell him I have to finish some paperwork. He goes into the living room, turns and asks if he can look at one of my books. He chooses a big picture book of old palaces, and sits on the couch, tucking one leg under him, the slanting light from the lamp making bright gold and shadows of his curly hair. I wash up the dishes, then sit at the cleared kitchen table with my stack of papers. Never once, when I look over at him, does he look up.

Later, I say it's time for me to go to bed. I get him a spare blanket and pillow. It feels too weird to offer him something to sleep in, so I don't. I tell him what time I have to leave in the morning, so he'll be ready.

Of course I find it almost impossible to sleep with him in the apartment. I lie in the cold bedroom, listening. Maybe I fall asleep for a little, but I wake up sharp and listen. I get out of bed, carefully cross the bare wood floor and put my ear against the door, warm from the heat in the other room. I go over to the window, watch the rain fall, listen to its grating on the glass. It's cold, I get back into the cold bed. I fall asleep, but wake again, listening. I get up, cross the icy floor, slowly ease the groan of the bedroom door.

He's lying on the floor, not the couch. One foot, with a saggy sock, pokes out from under the blanket. He's on his side, hugging the pillow. His hair in his eyes, his mouth loose, he's washed all over with the vibrating pink glow of the wall heater, sleeping in its electric hum. A young, sleeping alien in my small world.

I WAKE UP LATE. As I dash through to the bathroom for my shower, he's lying on the couch now, the blanket pulled up over his chin. But his eyes are open, and he lifts his head when he sees me. I tell him to eat anything he can find. When I come out of the bathroom, he's sitting forward on the couch, with his jacket on, ready to go. Beside him, the blanket is folded perfectly, the pillow smoothed and squarely placed on top of the blanket. He sits there, watching me, as I scramble after my shoes and my jacket. I grab my umbrella.

"Okay, gotta go!"

He gets his skateboard and we go out, I lock the door. We're quick down the stairs, down the front steps and out onto the sidewalk. I want to say something to him, I don't know what to say to him. I need to catch the streetcar.

"Hey, you take care, okay? You're a good kid. I hope it all works out, you know—I really gotta go! Take care!"

"Thank you." He says it plainly. I can't find any calculation or expectation in his tone. Only the lovely deep voice.

I'm down at the end of the block, turning the corner, when I look back. He's just putting his skateboard wheels-down on the sidewalk. He holds up his hand, palm facing, as a goodbye wave. I wave back large and turn the corner.

My workday is a mess. I'm too tired, I made a mistake in the paperwork, I have meeting after meeting all day, and I don't have time to think about the boy at all. But when I'm on the phone and at lunch, I can't seem to follow a conversation. Digits go missing from the long strings of numbers I add and subtract. I can't find the hole punch.

I'm exhausted during my trip home. Yet I strain to see who gets on at every streetcar stop. And with each face I search, the focusing just erodes my memory of the boy's face. Here, this thing happens to me and I can't even make a memory of it that doesn't shift and fade. My feet are a heavy scraping on the sidewalk, my three blocks home, just wanting to be home. I step off the sidewalk, into the courtyard.

And there's the kid, sitting on the front steps. He stands up. He's smiling, or trying not to smile. And I can't believe how happy I am to see him. Happy to see him standing there. Happy that he's trying not to smile.

I have to strain to lower, flatten the texture of my voice. "So, have I adopted you?"

He looks right into my eyes and smiles. And doesn't try not to.

AND THEN THE NEXT NIGHT. And the night after that. He waits for me, we eat. We watch movies, he looks at my books. He sleeps on the couch—or the floor—and folds away the bedclothes in the morning. I go to work and he goes away. And every night for a week now he comes back.

My apartment is so small. Four small rooms. There is barely enough room for me and my things, and yet he fits in so easily. When I make dinner, he walks around the apartment, asking me questions about everything, all the stuff I've crammed into this tiny space. He picks up each item, examines it, places it back exactly where he found it. A carved wooden box, an old tapestry pillow, a silver-plated bowl. Junk mostly. He'll carefully pull a book from a shelf, then put it back so precisely I'd never know anyone had moved it. He seems to recognize that everything fits just so, everything has its specific place. The chair, the bookcase, the umbrella, the watch taken off, the coat hung. He never disturbs anything. He makes no imprint.

I WONDER WHAT THE NEIGHBORS must think. What would I tell them if they asked me? How would I explain this teenage boy with a skateboard waiting on the steps for me to come home every night? This boy who doesn't live here. This boy who sleeps over at the apartment of a man who lives alone. How could I make them understand this friendship between a boy and a middle-aged man? When I'm that man, a man who currently finds his meager, calculated life centered around the comings and goings of a teenage boy. And you are that boy.

And what would I tell *you*? That you make me happy. That you make me confused. Am I in love with you? I don't know that I am, really. But maybe I'm in love with all the life that's still in you. Because most of the time it feels like my own life has somehow drained away. That I gave up or forgot how. But you always shake me out of that when you're here. Or when I think about you. But you, what would you say if I asked? What would you tell me if you could, if you let yourself tell me? Because the thing we don't acknowledge, the thing we pretend isn't there at all times, this question and maybe an answer, stammering between us, is *why*. Why did you follow me? Why do you come here?

I don't see him at first. It's pouring and, already wet through, he stands in the shadow under the porch by the door, not caring anymore if people ask him who he's waiting for. He laughs when I come up, safe under my umbrella, and when I grab his baggy, soaked jacket sleeve and drag him into the foyer.

We run in and then up the stairs. I turn the heater on full blast and he runs over to it, shaking loose from his jacket, dropping it, hopping on one foot then the other, yanking off his shoes. I get a towel and throw it to him. His shirt is wet through, and he laughs when he pulls at the soaked fabric, to show me how it clings to his skin.

He looks down at the floor, frowns, then strips the shirt off, too. I've never seen him without his shirt. His chest is smooth and white, but dark hair leads down his belly. I look away. He stands in front of the glowing, buzzing heater and shivers and laughs. Shivers and rubs the towel rough on his head, then his shoulders and chest. He turns one side then the other to the pink, rolling warmth of the heater. He laughs and turns to me, a bright, hard smile in his eyes, and twists the towel between his hands.

"You're hardly wet at all! Your stupid umbrella keeps you all dry!" He snaps the towel at me.

High school, gym class, sissy. He snaps it at me again, laughing. Because a snapped towel is only a game with this boy, a game you laugh along with. So I laugh along with the boy, and try to get the towel away from him.

He seems so much taller now, not a boy now. Shirtless and damp, turning and dancing and too quick for me. He twists and flings the towel out again, hard, and I catch the end of it with both my hands. He pulls back and we wrestle for it, stumbling, pulling hard on the towel, his face shining in the pink light, his wet hair swinging out away from his head. "Oh my God, you're *so* dry! You're *sooo* delicate—what a fag!"

High school, gym class, sissy. We stop, the towel pulled taut between us.

His breath in, pinched tight. The smile sits there stupid on my face.

He takes a step toward me. "No, I would never—I didn't mean—" He reaches toward my hand, barely touches his fingers along the cuff of my sleeve, then drops his hand away.

I say it quiet. "I know."

I let go my end of the towel. I take a step closer to him, crossing in front of the heater, the warmth of it curving across my back, the shadow of me taking all the light from his eyes and his skin. But when I reach up and push the tangled wet hair back from his forehead, his face is warm. His smooth, warm skin and the rough of my fingers.

And this is the moment.

"It's okay."

But then it isn't, not for him. We eat. We watch a movie. But he hardly says anything all evening, and he won't hold my gaze. When I say goodnight, I look at him full on when I say the word. I try to somehow show it in my eyes, to let him know that I'm okay, that it's all okay. He looks back at me, but I can't tell what's in his eyes, and he looks away.

I lie in bed, in my pajamas. I lie there in the cold bedroom, listening. I pull the covers up over my chin. I hear the hum of the heater on the other side of the wall, and along the bottom edge of the door, a thin line of pink light, but the warmth is only in there where the boy is.

I sleep. I don't know if I dream. The wind is muffled by walls and thin window glass, but rain still grates like sand on the window. Wind and streetlight and shapes of trees that slide and blur along the plain white walls. The shadows on a kind of delay, dragged along against the light, shadow crossing shadow. I lie in bed, facing the wall that separates me from the boy.

I sleep. I wake. The covers lift, a brush of cold air against my back. There is weight on the bed that isn't mine. Then heat that isn't mine. I turn as the boy moves beside me. I put out my hands, afraid, but where I touch is all skin and warm, his warm skin, and I pull my hands away. He drops his curly head into the space beneath my chin. The smoky smell of his hair and the hot dampness of his cheek against my throat. He clutches at my sleeves, pulling the fabric tight against my shoulders, and he murmurs something. His deep voice. He raises his head and looks at me. The light is behind him and I can't really see his eyes. He kisses my mouth before I can stop him. I try to hold myself away from him, but he kisses me with stupid, awkward boy kisses.

I'm in my pajamas because I'm no one's lover. He fumbles with my buttons, but I push his hands away. I lift my hand to his face, the sweat on his forehead, and brush his hair back. I want to see his eyes, I want a moment to find something more there in his eyes, but he wraps his arms up around my shoulders, lacing his hot fingers at the back of my neck. He pushes his head into my chest, his lips against my chest, the thin fabric between. And I can't help but touch him, then, touch his straining arms and his broad, smooth shoulders, the tightness at the small of his back. His arm comes down, he arches his back, and his hand rough at my waist, groping clumsy through the fabric. Fast down into my pajama bottoms, he takes me in his hand.

I turn away from him, grabbing his wrist, pull his hand away. With my elbows and feet I push myself quick to the edge of the bed. I drop down onto the floor, the sheets and blanket caught, pulled half off of the mattress. I kneel, turned away, twisted up in the blankets. I don't look at him. I won't look at him.

"You have to go back in the other room."

There's no sound. But now I hear his body release

itself slowly down into the bed. His head coming down, the sound of his hair spreading out on the pillow. The dry brush of his hand, his arm along the sheet, and the soft groan of the mattress as his body relaxes, unfolds. He makes a low noise in his throat, maybe a word. The bed shifts gently as he lifts himself again, then a dull creak and another as he turns, slides over, and gets up. He walks across the cold room, the sound of his feet patting on the cold wood floor. I don't look at him. I don't move. Except that I can't stop my eyes from tracing the heavy, twisting curve of sheet and blanket, the rising line that tethers me to the empty bed.

He stops by the door and turns to me. And I look up at him, now, standing naked in the waving tangle of tree and streetlight. His soft and hard young body, white where the light strikes it, whiter than the white wall, shadows curving and turning along his skin. His hair pushed back from his damp forehead, the shadows rising and falling across his face, across the light in his eyes. And he looks away. He makes that low sound again in his throat, maybe a word, and goes out, closing the door.

THE MORNING IS BRIGHT. The bright you only get late in the fall, when the leaves are all gone. The sun is a hard kind of bright, with nothing left to shade or deflect.

I get out of bed, and the floor is cold on my feet. The sound of my feet on the cold wood floor. I know before I open the door. He isn't in the living room. The blanket is folded neatly, perfectly, the pillow sitting squarely on top of the blanket. He isn't in the kitchen. The bathroom door is open. He isn't in the bathroom. I stand right outside my bedroom, still holding the doorknob, and I can see all this. My world is only this big and I can see it all. Everything is in its place, nothing is missing.

Except in the dish on the little table by the door, where I always leave it when I take it off, my watch is gone. It wasn't a new watch or nice at all, but the leather strap kept the curve of my wrist, and the inside lining, the thin leather lining that comes in contact with my skin, the sweat and perfume, smells of me.

1948

THE RAIN HAD STOPPED when he arrived, the sun come out. Above the gate was a small arched trellis, half climbed over and weighted with masses of fat yellow roses. The gate stuck and Carl was forced to give it a gentle shove. Then, bending to pass beneath the low trellis, the tall young man was caught by a drooping cluster of roses. Still soggy with rain, they shattered and fell, so that he arrived at the cottage door brushing water from his hair and off his clothes, yellow petals strewn about his shoulders, and with a small thorn scrape on his forehead.

A slight woman in a soft flower-printed dress and a lavender cardigan draped over her shoulders answered the door, her smile changing to concern.

"Oh, dear, the roses have got you! Come in. Let me get you a plaster."

"Oh, I'm sure it's nothing. Please don't bother."

"No bother. Just a moment."

She turned and disappeared through a doorway, leaving him standing awkwardly in the hall.

Carl had thought she would be rather a feeble old woman, the way the request had been presented to him by

Mr. Peters. He already knew her to be past sixty, which did seem rather an age to him. And there were broad streaks of silver in her ash-blonde hair. But this woman, brisk and sharp, wasn't at all his idea of an old woman.

She was quickly back and walked right up to him where he stood, reached up and softly brushed a wet strand of hair back from his forehead. Carl didn't know where to look, so aware of her closeness, this stranger, and her lovely, subtle scent. Lavender powder? Or jasmine?

"Just a moment." She pulled the little papers from the plaster, lifted it and gently pressed it over the thorn's scratch. Their eyes met then. Hers were a pale green, edged with russet brown. She looked at him without a hint of shyness and smiled.

"That should do it. Here, now, I've made tea." Gesturing toward the sitting room, "Please sit down, won't you? I'll bring it right in."

Carl sat stiffly on the sofa, knees drawn together, hands on knees. He looked about the room. Warm, cozy, pretty. Good furniture, but nothing very grand. Nothing frilly. A fireplace with an antique clock upon the mantle. Two oil paintings of rich green landscapes. And there was an old, framed photograph above a small desk. A good-looking young man in a uniform of the first war. Husband, brother? French doors led out onto a mossy, brick-paved terrace.

"Here we are." She put down the tray in front of the sofa and sat in the armchair opposite him. She leaned forward. "Shall I pour?"

"Yes, thank you Mrs.— "

"Please call me Marjorie."

"Marjorie," he echoed softly.

"And I'll call you Carl." She smiled at him over the

edge of her teacup. "You know, Mr. Peters led me to think you were a younger boy."

"Oh, sorry?"

Marjorie waved her hand to reassure him. "No, it's no problem. Not at all. But, out of curiosity, how old are you, Carl?"

"Nineteen."

"And you've not lived here terribly long, have you? Only about a year or so, if I understand correctly."

"That's about right. Ten months."

"And where before?"

"I spent two years in Guildford after leaving the camp school in Sayers Croft."

"Then you were evacuated during the war? From London?"

This was a topic Carl usually tried to avoid. "Yes, mum and dad saw me off right after the war began."

"That must have been hard; you were how young?"

Carl put down his tea on the table. "Just ten."

"Did they come for—"

"No, they both are dead." Carl picked up his tea cup again, turned to look out the French doors into the garden, almost embarrassed. "Right before the last of the Blitz."

"I'm so sorry. But any other family?"

"No, I'm afraid not."

"So you're all on your own, then."

Carl nodded. "Oh, but that's alright." He smiled slightly, to reassure her, trying to veer away from what always felt to him an awkward thread of conversation. "It's only that it's been a bit of a challenge, finding work and all, now that I'm finished with school. That's why I was so glad when Mr. Peters said you wanted someone to help look after things here. I've done rather a lot of gardening, and I'm fairly clever at fixing things. So I—"

"Why don't I show you."

Marjorie led him round the house, pointing out the things that needed mending. A crack in the plaster in the pantry, a dripping faucet in the kitchen, the second bedroom in much need of painting. Other small, simple things.

They returned to the sitting room.

"Are the arrangements satisfactory, then? Mr. Peters told you what I could pay?"

"Yes, it's all quite satisfactory, thank you."

"Good! Then you'll start next week, if that's agreeable?"

"Yes, next week."

There was an awkward pause, and Carl looked about the room, thinking he should find a way to say good day. He looked up at the photograph of the soldier again. Marjorie followed his glance.

"That was Bob, my husband. So handsome in his uniform."

"From the first war?"

"Oh, yes. It was taken during his last leave."

"If I might ask, how long were you married? Do you have any children?"

"Bob and I were married nine years before the war began. But no children. It just didn't happen for us. And then, of course, he didn't come back from the war…."

"I'm very sorry—"

Marjorie stood up suddenly, stepped to the French doors, turned and smiled, the sunlight streaming in behind her, her hair a bright halo.

"But I haven't even shown you the garden!"

1962

WITH THE MEDICINE FOR PAIN that the doctor had given her, Marjorie slept most of the day. With her hair all gone white, it was often only her small face that was clearly discernable in the midst of their white bed. The old house was draughty, wouldn't keep the heat, and Carl worked to keep a fire going in the bedroom grate all day and all night. Even then, it sometimes wasn't enough for Marjorie. She'd wake, turn her head to gaze at the flames, and whisper to Carl that she could see the fire but couldn't feel its warmth.

It was late in January, now, and a light snow had fallen.

Her voice was soft and hoarse. "Carl, I'm so cold. Won't you come and warm me, love?"

Carl slipped off his shoes and got into their bed, took her in his arms, wrapping himself carefully around her ever-smaller frame.

"No, like you used to, love," she whispered into his ear.

He knew what she meant, but he tried to dissuade her. "But it's just too cold for that. You'll be too cold."

"You'll make me warmer . . . Carl? . . . You'll make me warmer . . ."

And so he let her go and slid to the edge of the bed, bent down and pulled off his socks. His thick jumper, unbuttoned his shirt, took down his trousers and slipped out of his vest and underpants. He slid in next to her again, pulling up the covers.

Carl hesitated for a moment, but Marjorie turned and looked at him with such fierceness in her eyes. Something very different from the drugged blur he'd seen so often lately, that he'd almost become used to. Her gaze, now, was completely alert, focused.

"Go on, then," she said faintly but clearly and smiled. A smile as bright and full of love as it ever had been. A smile he'd rarely seen in all the hard and painful months that had come before.

He leaned in and kissed her cheek, at the same time starting to unbutton her nightgown. Beginning at her throat, the long, long row of tiny buttons. As he reached the last, she lifted her own hand and fumbled the nightgown open. Shaking and slow, her hand reached for his and placed it on her breast.

He'd only known her, loved her, known her body as that of a woman past middle age. In her sixties, in her seventies. She was so small now, wasted, after all the months of illness. But when he traced his warm hand along her soft and gently draping skin, smoothed over the delicate bones, he still found her almost shockingly beautiful. And as he pulled the covers back up around the two of them, brushed a wisp of hair from her pale cheek, he told her so.

"How beautiful you are, my darling girl. No one half as lovely . . ."

Her voice barely audible now, taking breath between words, "You still love me, then, my Carl?"

Afraid to let her see the tears he felt begin to break, he took her in his arms again, lifting her to him, covering her, pressed his chest against her chest, his hips against her hips, wrapped his leg over hers, kissed her face, her neck, again and again, cradled her head in his hand and stroked her hair.

His cheek pressed against hers, he whispered into her ear any sweet thing he could think to say, repeating himself, his throat going dry, afraid to let silence enter the room.

He held her like this, stroking her hair, whispering until, finally, he couldn't lie to himself any longer that she still heard him. That she breathed. That her body still returned anything of the heat of his.

The light was fading into evening, no lights on in the room, the fire finally abandoned and dying to embers in the grate. He slowly pulled back from her, took his arms from around her, wiped the blur of tears from his face with his palms. He pulled back the covers now to look at her body, the body he'd made love with countless times, the body of the woman he loved, the body that had let her go.

In the dimming light he reached out and touched her once more. He put his fingertips to her eyelids, traced her brows and along the bridge of her nose, trailed the line of her clavicle, her sternum, lifted and felt the scant weight of her empty, drooping breasts, he held her arm at the elbow, articulated the tiny, fragile wrist, cupped her arching hipbones, curved his fingers around her sex, smoothed her wasted legs. All cold.

He got up then, walked as he was—naked, this tall man of only thirty-three, his eyes dry now and clear—to the kitchen and took a small knife from the drawer. He returned to the bedroom, placed the knife on the bedside table, and got back into their bed. He lay there beside her, uncovered, the two of them naked. Naked, side by side, as they sometimes had lain on a warm summer evening.

But it was cold winter now. Carl reached over and took up the knife, held it, turned it in his hand, wondered at the degree of light it managed to catch even in that darkening room, paused when he caught a fragment of his own reflection. Then he brought it down and carefully traced the blade long, very lightly along the vein of his arm. Twice. And then, trying not to close his eyes with the fear and the pain, to close his eyes and botch the job, he pushed hard into the faint blue line and dragged the steel edge along the vein's path, until he could stand it no more. Until he'd done what he'd meant to do. Until his bright red blood ran hot at his side, ran in the narrow valley between their two bodies, spreading tendrils into the white sheet beneath them, soaking downward into the mattress they had shared for almost fourteen years.

Carl pulled the thin, white coverlet up and over the two of them, rested his head against Marjorie's shoulder, and went to sleep.

They were found in the morning only two days later. The fire long out, the bedroom was icy, the snow outside reflecting bright white into the room, only intensifying the whiteness of the sheets and pillow slips, the white of Marjorie's hair, the absence of color in both the dead faces. The only difference, the only warmth, was the rich brown of Carl's hair against the pillow and a thin line of crimson that marked a path between them on the white coverlet.

Exiles

I'VE WATCHED THE YOUNG MARQUIS all the long after-noon. Watched him as he strolls aimlessly, alone, through our wing of the château, past half-shuttered, richly curtained windows. Watched the color of his expansive red silk gown fade and brighten as he passes in and out of shadow and the narrow bands of light. I've watched how the substance of these rooms, the geometry and hue of things, is altered by his slow progress through the scant and granular sunlight, giving the briefest sensation of something alive, something waking, when in truth there's nothing more than his passing steps and the cold, inces-sant rustle of silk.

I've watched the sunlight pooling at the edges of the parquet. How the reflected light curves along the nearly translucent porcelain surface of a bronze-mounted Chinese vase, delineates each precious line in the carved leg of a gilded armchair. How it describes the delicate edges, the milky sheen of a marble bas-relief, the blue depth of a densely-embroidered velvet cushion, the glittering pink enamel of a jeweled snuffbox. I've watched as the marquis' soft fingers caress the beautiful surfaces of these objects, the exquisite ornaments that surround him here.

I've watched the young marquis all day as he's watched himself. Gazing at his own reflection in different mirrors, calculating how he looks from different angles, in different lights. He had a very confused hairdresser down from Paris this morning to make up that ridiculously elaborate coiffeur, all roses and ribbons, the feathers brushing against the tops of the doorways as the marquis parades contentedly from room to room.

I've watched as he made the hairdresser an extra payment to keep the visit a secret; does he really think the chatty little fellow capable of keeping the promise? Soon all Paris will know. Then how long before the duchesse de Langueuil comes again to argue with her son, before we have to listen to the metallic drone of her pleas, endure her ridiculous tears? But much worse if his father should come. He's been down only once since the marquis was sent here, and the argument then was terrible, the deep, rolling tremor of the military voice making the crystals of the chandeliers quiver and sway. It ended with him striking his son hard across the face, so hard the marquis was thrown to floor.

Later, the marquis was quite pained—more than on account of his father's rage, much more than his bloodied mouth—that when he fell, he knocked over a tiny inlaid table and the delicate edge of a *bronze doré* mount was bent. You see, he loves his beautiful possessions more than anything. More than any living thing.

When the young marquis arrived to take up his forced residence here, safely away from Paris and Versailles, the *marchand* arrived soon after. Conferring with the eager merchant, the marquis ordered new *boiseries* and carpets and whole suites of furniture for these rooms we share.

As the beautiful pieces began to arrive, so did the bills. Then more bills, then letters stamped with the duc's seal. But all remained unpaid, his father's heavy red wax seals unbroken. Until one day the frantic *marchand* had to explain that nothing more could be ordered, not a single thing more delivered. And so we have not been completely remade. The sofas that match the *fauteuils* never arrived, and the paneling remains ungilded.

In my time here, I have seen many different arrangements of the rooms in this wing, and I rather like this new half-completed décor. The empty places left in the ensemble; the little voids seem correct to me somehow. And I rather like this marquis, as well. I'm amused by his childish greed, his languor, his stupidity. It amuses me to watch this young man with all his pretty dresses and his mirrors. To watch him turning and posing, or drowsing in a chair, staring out from the window. Or dancing from one room to another, singing to himself. Tunelessly. For no one to hear, only his own deluded pleasure; we are always alone here, both of us fairly content to be. The few servants only come when called.

But there is a scarlet-headed bright green parrot that currently amuses the marquis. He is teaching it to speak, or believes that he is. The bird, being a bird, is distracted and the marquis will soon tire of it. And there is an old cat, deaf and nearly blind who, being a cat, refuses to recognize that it is unloved, and slowly follows the marquis from room to room.

I believe the marquis suffers little from his solitude. Surprising, given his former life, the frenzied and illicit amusement of nights and mornings in Paris. Before his parents were made aware and ashamed, before his banishment. But, really, I think the marquis doesn't much care for people—no, not at all—and that makes me like him all the more. So you see it is not only these rooms we have in common, not only this most comfortable of imprisonments.

You must know the marquis is unconscious of my presence, that I share these rooms. Of course I have every right to be here. At least as much as he; though separated by seven generations, we are of the same family. An old, important family. This estate, these lands have always been ours. And I lived my entire brief life in this château. Yes, I was born in Paris—far too early—where my mother had gone to visit her own mother, suddenly taken ill. My grandmother died and I was born. And only days later I was brought here; I was badly made and not expected to live.

My mother remained in Paris. I was her second son and would be the last of her children; three before me had died, one at birth, the other two in her womb. But I had an older brother, tall and strong and red-cheeked. From my window, I saw him on his gray dappled horse one day when he'd come out to hunt in the great park. I think I was ten; it was the only glimpse I ever had of him or any of my relations, that I can remember.

I was cared for by a series of girls and old women. No matter their age, they were all the same. The same fear in their eyes when they first saw me, bent and drooling as I was, the suppressed gasp and the held breath. Then their turning away, their whispers to the housekeeper. If they didn't leave right then, if they took me on—enduring my senseless babble, my frustrated shouts, the difficulty in feeding me, the constant cleaning I required—still, they never stayed long. Good Christians, all, they rarely looked me in the eye, and when they did, would quickly cross themselves.

I was cared for then, in the simplest sense of the word, but otherwise ignored. They all thought me an idiot. Because I couldn't speak, because I couldn't walk or care for myself, I wasn't taught to read or to do anything at all. What they didn't understand, though, is that I saw well enough. And heard quite the better. And because they never considered me, were completely unguarded in my presence, I witnessed all the awful, stupid things they did, heard their lies. I knew it all. They saw me as weak and feeble, but I saw that they were so much worse off than I. My weakness was only a question of mechanics, they were weak in their minds and in their souls. I found them pathetic and had no pity for them.

I managed seventeen years in that twisted, decaying body. On account of stubbornness, I suppose; I merely lived to spite them all, to keep them at the tasks they found so unpleasant. But now everything is so much simpler. I know no struggle. Accustomed to my lack of speech, I've never missed it after. And over time—all this time—I've only learned to see yet more clearly, to hear yet more precisely. And I have no limitations, now, within the limitation of these rooms. If I understood what it meant to be happy, I might say that I am happy to rest here. Happy, now, to watch my distant kinsman, this silly young man in his silly gowns, and to have seen all those who came here before he did, all who hid here, too. All who were hidden.

THE DARK GREEN SILK CURTAINS in the *petit cabinet* never got their gold braid trim. It makes the marquis fuss and mutter when he sees them. But I think it's lovely the way the afternoon sunlight shines through them, washing green along the walls, settling green along edges, within corners. Just now, as the marquis enters the room, approaching the window, the brush of his skirts on the floor, bright then soft as he moves from polished parquet to carpet, the sunlit red gown of the marquis makes a sharp contrast with those same green curtains. And with the green bird as well, which he holds aloft into the light of the window. The old gray cat comes in from the shadows, sits slowly, rises again slowly, creeps a few steps closer, sits again.

I think the old cat is afraid of me, really. It turns away from me always, pretends it doesn't see me. But the marquis' bird is fascinated by my presence and stares at me. The marquis thinks the bird repeats all the newly taught words for his benefit, but he has never understood why the bird always turns his head this way or that as he speaks his learned words. He assumes it's a quirk of talking birds.

Standing in the window, the light in his eyes, the marquis confers with the bird. More instruction. Unimaginative, charmless phrases, repeated and repeated. The bird opens its beak, turns its head, the feathers of its thick neck ruffling, fanning out with the turning. The tilted, swiveled head, the flat black eyes gazing in my direction. The marquis follows the bird's gaze, straining to see into the shadows of the room. The green bird attempts a new word, his thick black tongue rising in his beak, a word never taught him by the marquis. A name, actually, unknown to the marquis. Quietly at first, tentatively, but then louder, the green bird utters this untaught word. He repeats it again, and then again, my name.

Two brothers

1952

THERE IT IS, he whispered to himself, out loud, and stopped, standing in the middle of the road, focused on the line of trees up along the ridge of the hill.

That moment not long before the sun climbs up from the back of the hill, a few scarce seconds when the soft light through the branches seems to flicker slightly, to vibrate, the silent gray humming into a thin edge of pink or orange, before it all goes calm again. It was this particular moment that he always hoped to see when he was out so early, long before anyone back at the house was up.

As he continued down the road, the light grew warmer, richer every second, the silence receding. Birds were singing now. Different pitches, different rhythms. Staccato and legato, words from the piano lessons he took when he was little. He used to know so many of the birds' songs, but they all seemed to knot up together now, and he couldn't tell one from another. There was an insistent beat of one bird's song that almost aligned with the grit of his footsteps on the pavement. He tried to match it with his gait, but it kept going out of sync.

His walk to the lake had been a crazy zigzag, as he'd tried to avoid the new housing tracts. Before the war, this area and all the way past the lake used to be very private, exclusive. Old families, big houses hidden in the woods down long driveways. His grandfather, his mother's father, had been furious when developers started buying up parts of the county. And now, scattered among what used to be unspoiled, wooded countryside, there were tight treeless clumps of squat houses and concrete sidewalks.

But he was beyond the tangle of new houses, now, and his path had returned to the one long, shaded road that stretched to the lake.

He remembered how it used to be, when he was little. How they'd drive down this same road when the weather was warm. When it was summer, especially, when it was very hot, when they got to that last part, where the paved road ran out, and he could smell the grass and pine and wildflowers warm from the sun, the scent of them even in the dust coming up from the road. The big car going slow over that rutted dirt road, each wheel seeming to step carefully in and out of every pothole. And moments later, he and his little brother would be out of the car, navigating the wide arc of sun-hot rocks at the lake's edge, forced to go too slow over the uneven and burning stones, while both of them just wanted to run as fast as they could for that first splash into the cool water. Like the way the car had had to inch along in low gear, when its powerful engine longed to roar with speed.

The sun having climbed over the edge of the hill, now, the morning light quickly descended through the treetops, sifted down though their branches, settled into the shrubby hills and spread its way across swathes of tall grass, mossy rock, tangled vines, day reclaiming every variation of green.

He heard the break of a twig, stopped and turned, as a young doe raised her head out of the brush and caught sight of him. She stared, nose quivering, ears twitching. He held his breath, didn't move. The doe didn't move, either, just stared at him, her beautiful eyes not blinking. In the slowing seconds they held this connection. But then something in the blank directness of her gaze made him think about what he didn't want to think about, made him think about what happened with Randy. Randy Glazer. And he made a step toward the doe, waving his arms, and she bolted as he called out, Go!

WALKING BACK FROM BASKETBALL practice that night three weeks ago, and the two of them are laughing in the dark, shooting the ball back and forth between them. Can you believe the look on Coach's face when Hoskins missed that shot? Then, like in a game, the one protecting the ball is using his back, his hip to shove the other away. I know, I thought he was gonna have a conniption! Then pretending to fight, arm punching, shoulder butting. You gonna block like that when we play Sacred Heart?

Beyond the streetlights now, down the wooded road toward their houses, and Randy, still talking, both of them laughing, side by side, puts his arm around Willy, his hand on Willy's shoulder. Still laughing, he moves his hand smooth up the side of Willy's neck, ruffles his hair, then leaves his warm fingertips curved loose along Willy's throat.

The laughing fades into the sounds of the night. And Willy doesn't pull away. The two boys walking along like this in the dark, their shallow breathing. All either can know, now, is the exact location of that unforeseen touch, the shock of its warmth. Their walking this way, linked together, gradually goes out of sync and Randy, too far to the side, steps off the pavement into the dirt beside the road, pulling Willy with him. Willy stumbles and both boys fall down into the long grass, beneath the trees, out of the moonlight.

After, they hunt for the basketball. Randy, brushing the hair out of his eyes, laughs, That was kind of crazy. He tries to catch Willy's gaze in the dark, Crazy, huh? but Willy won't look at him.

He reaches for Willy's arm, Hey, say something. Willy pulls away, finds the ball in the tall grass, stiffly, wordlessly hands it to Randy without looking him in the eye, turns and walks quickly toward home. Randy calls after him, Hey, Willy, wait up. Then, Are you mad? But Willy breaks into a sprint and is soon lost into the dark.

He tries to avoid Randy at school, fakes a muscle strain to get out of basketball practice. But three days later, coming around a corner in the road through the woods, they come face to face. Willy freezes, turns to walk away again.

But Randy says, Come on, Willy, wait up, don't be that way. It just happened, it doesn't mean anything. Willy looks at the ground. But Randy steps forward, whispers, It's okay, nobody will ever know. You think I'd tell anyone? It's just us. Talk to me.

They go and sit by the side of the road, a one-sided conversation with Willy looking at the ground, looking off into the trees. Until Randy touches Willy's hand, and Willy finally turns and looks at Randy. And the seconds while they hold each other's gaze is something Willy can't even understand, so painful and sweet and free.

In the following days it makes Willy a confused sort of happy to have this secret, not thinking beyond now. No one would suspect anything, anyway. They've been friends, they're on the team. And so something releases inside of him, just thinking only for now.

Then, only days later, leaving English class, Willy meets Randy by his locker. Randy has a new flattop. Like he said he would. Willy laughs and says, You said you would, and runs his hand just above the precise horizontal of it. Still laughing, his hand gripping Randy's shoulder, he turns and, across the hall, Marjorie Everett is watching the two of them, her cat-eye glasses and her red lip-sticked mouth, a strangely blank expression on her face. Marjorie, who he's known all his life. And under the focus of her gaze, an awful heat rises from his throat, flushes into his cheeks. Marjorie Everett keeps staring at him, the red circle of her mouth. He tries to smile at her, to shrug, to lie her away from any understanding, but he's frozen by the sickening heat. He turns away from Randy, almost knocking his books out of his hand. Without a look back, without a word, he jogs down the hall to his next class. He can barely find the classroom door with the heat risen behind his eyes.

And then, when Randy calls the house, Willy won't take the call. Randy slips a note in Willy's locker, a note that Willy doesn't answer. Willy skips practice, starts skipping school, trying to avoid Randy. And everyone. Because he can't look at anyone now, too afraid to see in their gaze what they might see in his. He knows that he'll never be able to hold those blank stares. And he knows he can't go back to where he was before, can't step forward into what he knows now.

THE BOY REACHED THE END of the well-maintained pavement, where only a dirt road had always continued, hard-packed and deeply rutted. Before long he saw far ahead the great arch of tall trees that opened onto the beach and the lake just beyond view. That portal of green, the woods giving itself up to sand and rock and water always seemed some sort of magic to him when he was a small boy.

He walked a little faster then. And as he reached the arch of trees, stepping through to that width of blue sky, everything was as beautiful as it ever had been, maybe even more so. He walked out onto the sand, slipped off his shoes, his socks. The sand was cool on the soles of his feet, cooler still as his feet sank in the sand as he walked. There was still a chill in the air this early in the day, but he reached down and pulled up his shirt, over his head, and let it fall behind him. He tensed as the cool breeze brushed along his skin.

Hemming the water's edge was a wide heap of worn-smooth rocks, most large, some immense. In the summer of all his memories, the rocks were fiercely hot from the sun beating down on them all day. The final passage into freedom—getting from the warm sand to the cool water—was the trial of having to run over those burning stones.

He climbed up onto the first wide, nearly flat rock and it was cold under his feet. The breeze off the lake ruffled his hair. Looking out at the water, he reached two fingers down into the coin pocket of his jeans and found the small knot of white paper. Blue ink on a corner of lined white notebook paper.

He took out the note, folded tight, almost enough to make it disappear, the note that Randy had left in his locker, and held it clenched in his fist. He stared down at his fist, watched his fingertips turn pink, gripped hard around the unread note—a note he couldn't, hadn't allowed himself to read—and then flung it far out in the water, where he knew the blue ink would bleed away, the paper washed blank, dissolving.

He stepped forward along the cold rocks, unbuttoned his jeans, slid them off, slid off his shorts. Stepped up onto one of the largest rocks, the highest one, and turned back, looking toward the green shadow of woods, the bright sand. Then to the vast break of gray stones that arched away from either side of where he stood.

He closed his eyes, felt the sun, the ever-warming breeze on his face, in his hair, along the length of his young body.

Opening his eyes to scan the clear and empty sky, he turned once again, gazed down at the calm greenish water, and stepped forward, descending to the lake's edge. The water would be cold, he knew.

1954

AFTER WHAT HAPPENED WITH WILLY, my parents sent me up to Chawton Hall. They were having a really hard time. Mother wasn't sleeping. But she was drinking a lot. Dad stayed in the city most of the time. And they didn't know what to do with me. Honestly, I think they'd always seen me as the extra son, the spare. That sounds funny, I guess, but it was always Willy they were so proud of, the first born, the one they expected so much of. And now there was just me.

Anyway, someone told them it would be good for all of us if maybe I went away to school. At least for a while. I was only there for two terms. Chawton's a boy's school. A prep school. I had never been away from home before. I didn't know anyone there. I was shy and pretty lonely, I guess. And I met another boy who didn't know anyone, who was lonely. Tommy was from Vermont, and had shiny black hair and freckles and big, dark brown eyes. And we fell in love. Or whatever it was. This was last fall, so I was fifteen and he was only fourteen, so what do I know. But it felt like love. More than I ever thought it would feel like. We knew that it was queer to feel that way, but we didn't know what to do. And it made us too happy to want to stop. But one time, when we thought we were safe, someone saw us, I don't know, kissing, and told on us. I think it was Jimmy Dennison, but I can't prove it. Then people—the head-master, my father and Tommy's mother, who both came up—sat us down and started asking us questions, and we didn't know what to say. We couldn't say anything. What could we say? So I had to leave school and come home. I don't know about Tommy. He went home, too, I figure. Maybe I'm stupid, but I'm going to try and send him a letter one of these days.

If you say that this isn't that big of a deal, that it could still be a phase, maybe, that boys really do often grow out of this kind of thing, I have to tell you there have been other things, too. Things I've done. Scott Bascom and I did stuff when we were in second grade. And Chuck O'Brien always liked to go out with me in the woods and compare things, if you know what I mean. I think it's so funny that now, all these years later, neither one of them will even look me in the eye when they see me in town.

But even before all that, when I was a real little kid—four or five—I had this sort of thing for Mr. Raskin, the gardener. I would follow him all around the property. I loved to watch him digging in the dirt, planting things. Or working on the lawn mower, with grease on his hands. I loved his grass-stained coveralls and the smell of his cigarettes and the smell of his sweat. I was only a little boy, and I didn't really know what I was doing, but I knew I wanted something from him, even if I didn't know what. Everybody thought it was so cute, but that's because nobody understood.

And there was this one day when I snuck out to his little house way out at the end of the property. It was a really hot summer day. I wasn't supposed to wander that far on my own. And—this is pretty queer stuff—I hid in the shrubs outside his bedroom window and watched him as he undressed, as he stood there in his room and rubbed a wet washcloth over his grown-up body. I'd never seen a man naked before, and I can still remember exactly the way it made me feel, that fluttering and sinking in my belly. I can remember thinking that it was probably wrong to have that weird feeling in my body, but I still liked it. But then Mr. Raskin turned and saw me at the window. He grabbed a towel, rushed over to the window before I could untangle myself from the bushes, and yelled at me to stay away from there and never do that again. He looked really, really mad. But also kind of scared. And he sure scared me. I ran for the house and kept away from him after that.

Since what happened with me up at school, I'm pretty much here all the time. At the summer house. So I have a tutor here, to finish up my high school stuff. His name is Mr. Heinrich, and he's German. Well, he was born there, anyway. Which seems kind of strange, to have a German tutor, what with the war and all. He's nice enough, and hardly has any accent. He's only been here three months so far, and kind of stiff, so we don't know him too well yet. When Mother and Father aren't here—which is most of the time—that just leaves us and Mrs. Larkin, the cook, and Barbara and Mary who take care of the house, cleaning and things. None of them pay much attention to me. When there's nothing to do, they sit around and smoke and read magazines. So, you see, it's pretty quiet here.

We used to have people come and stay the weekend all the time, Mother and Dad's friends, but nobody's come for a long time, now. Not since Willy died. I guess people are kind of creeped out being around people who've had someone in their family die. Especially when it's a kid. Even Mother and Dad don't come out often. They spend almost all their time in the city, now, even in the summer; we have a house in the city, too. When they *are* here, it's kind of tense. They try to act like everything's normal. But I catch them staring at me, not saying anything, and it makes me really uncomfortable. Because I know what they're thinking. That I'll never be like Willy, and that they still don't know what the heck they're going to do about me.

I don't know what I'm going to do about me, either. Still haven't decided what I'm going to do once I'm through with school. I suppose I'll have to go to college. If I'm still not so infamous they won't let me in. That's a joke. But I've probably got some sort of reputation now. "How sad for the Langfords, they lost one son and the other's a dirty queer." That's kind of a joke, too. But not really.

But it *is* kind of funny, honestly. The thing is, what I'm trying to say is, because I'm such a disaster, it's like nobody is going to expect anything from me. Not now. Maybe it would even be better for everyone if I wasn't hanging around. And, you know, I guess that's okay with me. Or better than okay. So when I'm done with all this tutoring business, get my diploma, maybe I can get away with skipping college. That's kind of a nutty idea, I guess, but maybe my folks will let me travel. They can afford it. I could travel for years and years—Italy, Egypt, Japan—seeing all sorts of things. And then I'd be out of their hair, wouldn't be the big embarrassment. Gradually, anyone who heard about what happened up at Chawton would maybe just kind of forget about it, forget about me. Out of sight, out of mind, you know. I'll move to a different state, different part of the country. Where people don't know me, where I can figure out what I want to do with my crazy life. Free to be who I want to be, who I am. I don't know, but that sounds alright to me.

Drop

THE PAIN IN HIS BAD KNEE, as he lifted his foot on and off the brake pedal. Inching along, heading north on the 5. Traffic had been moving slowly enough already. But now, at the point where the freeway split into three—downtown, the 405, the Marquam Bridge—everything had all but stopped. He lifted his foot and the car moved about five feet toward the bridge. His foot down and then only another five feet. He changed the radio station.

The car moved forward a few yards, then the twinge in his knee as he pressed down on the brakes. Then off again. Then on. He was finally starting that long sloping turn onto the bridge. He hated that bridge. The top deck was too open, the barrier at the edge too low. The road surface was tilted and the slope too steep. And he always had to quickly merge through several lanes of traffic to get from the far left lane over to the far right one so he could make his exit. Whether traffic was fast or slow, it always made him nervous.

He started to move forward again, but a shiny black SUV, pushing ahead of its place in line, wedged itself into his lane. Why did people have to act that way?

And why did his father have to be clear across town? It was already almost forty-five minutes since he'd left the nursing home. When they moved the old man out of his house, his sister had insisted they choose a place near her in Tigard. Because she was the one he'd always been closest to, she said. And then she never visited him. At least that's what the nurses said. He and his father had never been close, not anything like it, and now the old man was deep in dementia. But he went and sat with his father twice a week. Because it's what you do. And then he always got stuck in rush-hour traffic on the way back. He had less than a quarter tank of gas.

The car engine revved for no apparent reason. His great fear with all the extra driving he'd had lately was that the car would decide to die on the freeway or, even worse, a bridge. He couldn't afford a disaster like that. His Social Security was nothing. His retirement savings was nothing. Rent in his apartment went up every year. He'd had to give up his cable because he couldn't afford it anymore. What would he do if anything happened to the car?

He was just now approaching the upturn in the onramp's curve. Before too long the other lanes would join with his and he'd have to start the merge over to the other edge of the bridge. The grind of the ancient Corolla's brakes seemed to be the voice of the pain in his knee. Had to be more than arthritis, more than old age. Why didn't he go to a doctor, see what it was, see if they could do anything?

But why bother, he'd say, trying to fix a man of seventy-two, almost seventy-three. His wife left him twenty-six years ago. He hadn't seen his daughter in almost as long. He was stuck with the father who had never shown him any affection at all, and now didn't even know who he was. He didn't have any money, didn't have any friends. This was how he'd ended up, the life that every choice he'd made had led to. His bum knee was one thing, but how do you fix any of the rest?

The car slowly made the long slope up to the bridge's upper deck, stop by stop. He waited now right near the top of the onramp. He fussed with the radio station. And then through the windshield, with the angle of the car pointing up and the angle of the roadway pointing down, all he could see was the broad curve of blue sky.

EVERY SUMMER UNTIL WALTER was eleven he spent with his cousins at the lake. His parents would call a truce to their constant fighting, send him to his cousins at the lake, and go off together for "alone time," apparently trying to shore up their relationship. But every end of summer, when they came to pick him up, nothing seemed any different. When he was eleven his sister was born, and there were no more summers at the lake. The next year his parents divorced.

His aunt and uncle had money. His cousins had friends. And even though they were almost the same age as he was, they didn't want anything to do with him, thought he was boring, embarrassing. They made fun of him because he was fat and still wet the bed sometimes.

His last summer at the lake was no different than the ones that came before. His cousins teasing him, ignoring him, going off with their friends. His aunt asking wasn't he bored doing nothing, it was such a pretty day out, why didn't he go hang out with his cousins and their friends at the beach. "They're all such nice kids!"

He didn't like to go swimming. Though nobody else seemed to care, he thought the lake was too cold. And he didn't want to take his shirt off. He always wore a t-shirt when he went swimming, because he was embarrassed to be fat. But wearing a shirt at the beach was almost as bad.

One very hot day, though, after his aunt kept bugging him to do something, to go have fun—"It's summer!"— he changed his jeans for his swimsuit and went down to the lake. His cousins and their friends were there and easily made it very clear he was not welcome to join them. So he kept walking, like that's what he meant to do all along, walking away from the crowds. The yelling, splashing children, their mothers, flat on their backs, glistening with suntan lotion, the sun reflecting hard off their black sunglasses.

He walked along the water's edge, then away, sand caking his wet feet, thick between his toes, until he reached the narrow path leading away from the beach. He walked a little farther and came to a place where a large tree grew straight up between the path and the water. It hung out over the lake, its roots, the soil eroded by the slow lap of waves, stretched out naked right below the surface.

He sat down, put his feet in the water, swished the sand from his feet. The water was warmer than he expected, so he scooted down the bank and walked carefully among the slippery tree roots. His arms stretched out for balance, he walked just a little farther into the lake, the water reaching his waist now, his t-shirt floating up at first, then the water soaking the fabric, pressing it to him.

He stepped forward and slipped, the roots having given way to open water, deeper than he knew. He fell all the way in and down, his head under water, going down. He beat his arms and legs hard, trying to right himself, trying to get back up, trying to get his head out of the water, but he couldn't. The back of his t-shirt was snagged on a tree root but he didn't know it.

He kept struggling, his eyes wide open, trying to find whatever it was that kept him under. The water was cold and dark, down in it. All he could see was the sunlight coming through the branches of the tree above him, beyond the water, the patches of light shifting, growing larger and smaller, stretching and shrinking with the soft motion of the waves. And he could see the bubbles rising into that light, bursting at the surface, a bright, instant pinpoint of sunlight at each moment of contact and release.

But he wasn't struggling anymore, his arms stretched up, open toward the light. And it wasn't cold anymore. He didn't see the bubbles anymore. Just the shifting light, the sunlight sinking into the green water, making it blue like the sky. And it was bluer now. It was so blue.

Then a heavy shadow was over him, blocking the sun, a change of pressure in the water, in his ears, all at once. And then the tearing of the back of his t-shirt was something he thought he could hear. And then at the surface, a loud opening and a slamming shut, the weight of air.

Walter lay on the bank, not moving, the ripped t-shirt twisted around his middle, his soft, pink belly exposed. He'd thrown up all the water, and now that his coughing had slowed down, the man who had happened to see him go under, the man who'd run to him, pulled him out by his arm and by his hair, kept asking, "Are you alright, kid? . . . What's your name? . . . Are your parents on the beach? . . . Are you okay?"

But Walter didn't move, didn't say a word to the man, just stared up at him. His wet face pale, his eyes blank.

COMING UP ONTO THE UPPER deck of the bridge, he started trying to merge, kept looking over his shoulder, trying to find an opening. He made it over one lane and then his foot down on the brake pedal again. The grating of the brakes, the pain in his knee.

He turned and looked for another opening, turned back, rubbing his stiff neck. His turn signal was on, had been on, but no one would make space for him. He started edging over anyway, and the guy behind him in the next lane in the oversized pick-up honked and flipped him off. He could see the guy in the rear-view mirror yelling at him.

He had one more lane to get over. Turn signal still flashing, he kept looking back to see if he could make it. Starting and stopping, he finally began moving into the far-right lane. The radio was grating on his nerves, bad news on every channel, and he reached down quick to turn it off.

But right then, his foot slipped off the brake pedal, he moved quick to get it back, but then the sharp pain in his knee was too much to hold it and the car lurched forward, and his hand slipped on the radio knob, turning the volume all the way up. He was just on the downside of the bridge's arch, and the car started to veer back into the lane on the left. He turned the wheel sharply but overcorrected and rammed into the concrete barrier at the edge, scraping along hard for several yards before he could stop.

THE CAR SAT at an angle blocking the lane, and people started honking, tried to get around it, turning their wheels hard left, trying to push their way out from behind. People in the other lanes slowed down to look, saw the man just sitting in the car, heard the radio blaring.

The car door finally opened and the man got out, moving slowly. He stood for a long time, holding onto the door, staring at the other cars, some stopped, some moving, every face in every car turned toward him. The radio louder than anything, but it didn't seem like he noticed any of it.

He walked away from the car, the door left open, walked the few steps to the edge, the spray of glass from the broken headlight crunching beneath his feet. He looked down at the river so incredibly far below, the sunlight shining on the fast rippling water. He scanned the huge width of sky, above and all around. On the edge of the bridge, so high above the river and the land, there was nothing else but sky.

He turned around and sat down on the concrete barrier. People were yelling at him now. They were angry, confused, scared. Most were in cars, stopped or slowing, not knowing what was happening, or knowing what to do. The radio still blared. A woman had gotten out of her car and started to come closer, but stopped, and stood at a distance saying something. All the noise and all these people, and he just stared at them, his face pale, his eyes blank.

And then he smiled. He laughed. Then he laughed again. He raised his arms over his head, open, and tilted his head all the way back, his eyes wide open, taking in the bright blue sky. And in the same moment, in the same movement, he fell backwards from the edge, his feet coming up over his head, his face down, and he saw again the river so far below, the pinpoints of light, hard and miraculous, on the blue green water.

Miss Maureen

Nobody would say Maureen was a pretty woman. Too skinny, too tall. And she hadn't got a shape. Big hands and feet. She might have had a nice enough face, but you couldn't tell from the makeup, more makeup than people thought was proper. They said, this is Cedarville, this ain't Hollywood. How you gonna get a man looking like that, your face all painted up like Miss Greta Garbo or Mar-leen Dietrich?

She'd showed up in town a few years back, said she'd come from Louisiana, though she didn't sound it. But these were hard times, everybody out of work, looking for a way back up or a way out. So you didn't ask too many questions about where people came from or how they got where they got. Truth was, she'd only stopped in Cedarville because the money'd run out, as far west as she could make it. She'd considered herself lucky, then, to get a job waiting tables at the café down on Monroe Street. She was clean and quiet, smart, and she worked hard, so they were glad to have her. But she was just getting by, could barely save up a dime. Five years on and almost forty, she couldn't see how she'd ever make it to California now.

Maureen stayed up at old lady Ralph's boarding house. That Mrs. Ralph could be a terror. Like the way she'd holler and run off any Okies passing through, coming by her back door looking for a handout. But Maureen kept to herself, paid her rent on time, and the old woman let her be.

Maureen had her own room there. A narrow bed with worn-out springs, a washstand, a chair, a clothes cupboard was all it was. But she'd made it something like hers; a paper lantern printed in pink and red roses put up over the ceiling bulb, a bit of old lace-edged batiste she'd found and draped over the curtain top, a little green satin pillow, Chinese embroidered, which was always the last thing placed on her made-up bed each morning. And all her movie magazines.

ON HER DAYS OFF, Maureen would catch the bus into Albuquerque to go see the pictures. Most days, she'd make it there early enough for a matinee and stay through till she had to catch the last bus back to Cedarville. Sometimes, when she'd worked breakfast and lunch and had the night off, she'd head to town just to catch the evening show. These were the days when anyone who could afford a ticket would go to the pictures, to forget about real life, to dream of something better. And Maureen needed to dream at least as much as anyone.

She never liked the stories about bootleggers or cowboys. The ones she liked were the romantic ones, where the actresses were dressed in satin gowns, diamonds and furs. She lived each week to be able, in the dark of the movie house, to dream of being Garbo or Kay Francis or Norma Shearer. Or Joan Crawford, who always started out in a factory or a shop or a crummy diner—just like Maureen—before she rose to become a real lady, shimmering and spangled. She ached to live those movie lives.

To be immaculate and soft, to have Gable or Gary Cooper take you in his arms, to have him kiss you. Anything was worth that, even if you had to lose it all before you got it back in the end, even if you died before the fade out.

And when she got back to Mrs. Ralph's, late, having to get up early for work the next morning, she'd sit in the dim pink and red light of her room and try to hold onto something of that magic flickering up there on the screen. But it was hard enough to do, looking in the mirror as she pinned her hair up for the night. As she washed off her makeup, the black smudge of mascara smearing into the lines around her eyes, the chapped lips stained with lip rouge, the rough shadow along her jaw line. Hard enough to do.

ONE OF MAUREEN'S FAVORITE customers at the café was Mr. Anders, the principal at the school in town. He always called her "Miss Maureen." Even though he was actually probably a few years younger than she was, he seemed almost middle aged, with the soft hint of a belly beneath his vest. He was also about an inch or so shorter than Maureen. But he had the loveliest bright green eyes. They always seemed to catch the light, always seemed to be smiling even when he wasn't.

He ate there most breakfasts and suppers. The café was small, and Maureen and Mr. Anders usually carried on a conversation while he ate and she went about her work. Over the five years, they'd never talked about anything important or personal. But they had a sort of easy friendship, light and joking, but proper and respectful.

Maureen knew that he lived alone, in the house he'd grown up in; his father had died when he was a boy and his mother had passed away a few years back. He'd never married. If she had let herself think it, she might have seen that she had feelings for him. But those were the kind of thoughts she never let herself have. Not with the way things were. Even so, she wondered if maybe his feelings for her were stronger than friendship. He never spoke with the other waitresses the way he did with her, not even Florence, whom he'd known since they were children. And she couldn't help but notice the way he seemed to light up around her, the way he looked at her sometimes. Like he was looking right into her, like he understood more than she wanted him to. The kind of looking that should have scared her to death, the kind to make her pack her bags and move on. But all she could ever really find in the way he looked at her was kindness.

HE CAME IN FOR SUPPER earlier than usual one spring evening, just as Maureen was leaving for the day.

"So I shan't have the pleasure of your company, Miss Maureen?"

"No, can't say you will, Mr. Anders. I'm going into town to catch the new Claudette Colbert picture."

"Well, what do you know about that! I came in for supper early just so I'd have time to drive over and see that one, myself. You know, if you'd like, I'd be happy to drive you."

Maureen didn't know what to say. A man had never offered to drive her anywhere.

"Quicker than the bus!"

"That's awful nice of you, Mr. Anders, but I ain't dressed right, and I have to change, so—"

"Well, that's perfect. I'll just have a quick supper and then I can swing by and pick you up. If you'd like, that is. You're at Mrs. Ralph's, aren't you?"

"Well . . . I guess that'd be alright. Why, thank you, Mr. Anders. Yes, Mrs. Ralph's."

SHE WAS STANDING on the porch when Mr. Anders drove up and got out of the car, the motor running. He held the door open for Maureen. He told her to call him Ben.

"And how nice you look. I always expected you'd have an eye for the latest styles."

She felt foolish that he'd say such a thing. She thought what a right scarecrow she looked. Her clothes were old, her heels worn down, one of the fingers of her best gloves was starting to fray. Everything about the situation was embarrassing to her, and all the way into town she could barely choke out a word. Ben made up for it by talking about everything he could think of and didn't seem to notice—or pretended he didn't—just how uncomfortable she was.

Maureen finally started to relax once the lights went down and the picture started. The story wasn't much, but Colbert's gowns were so beautiful, so daring. And Maureen, as always, couldn't get over how low the actress' voice was, almost like her own. And by the time they left the theater, sharing their thoughts about the film, they were talking like old friends again.

"Miss Maureen, Prohibition ended more than six months ago, and I'd bet anything that neither of us has taken any opportunity to enjoy this new freedom. It's still early; would you be so bold as to join me in a glass of wine before I escort you home?"

There was a little restaurant right across from the theater. Turned out there was exactly one bottle of wine in the whole place—and it was awful. But they laughed and drank it anyway. They talked and talked; it was so easy to be together now. She couldn't remember ever being so comfortable with anyone, more free to be herself.

They had a second glass of wine. And after a bit, the waiter emptied the last of the bottle into their glasses and left them alone.

"Miss Maureen, I don't believe I ever asked you what brought you to Cedarville. Where are you from, anyway?"

Maureen looked down into her glass, only a drop or two of wine and then the dregs.

"Oh, you know, I don't much like to talk about that; is that alright, Ben?"

And it was.

IT WAS AFTER MIDNIGHT when the car pulled up to the boarding house. All was quiet but the porchlight was still lit. All was quiet in the car, too. That nervous quiet when people feel so much but don't know what to say to each other.

Ben turned toward Maureen—his green eyes flashing in the bright of the porchlight—and she studied his face as he looked to find the right words. Finally, he laughed, then his voice low and soft.

"Maureen, dear, I just want to tell you what a truly lovely time I've had in your company tonight. You're just about the nicest person I know. I hope we can do this again very soon."

He looked down, fussed with the crease in his trouser leg, then looked up with a shy smile.

"And I promise no more white lies about planning to see a picture I wasn't really planning to see. You knew I was fibbing, didn't you?"

They both laughed. And again Maureen didn't know what to say. Everything in her should have told her to get out, tell him goodnight and get out of the car. Instead, she let herself wait for whatever came next. She wanted whatever came next.

He took her hand in his. My rough hands, she thought. With his other hand he brushed her hair away from her cheek, leaned in and kissed her.

She had never been kissed.

It wasn't like in the pictures. It wasn't like anything she understood. He wasn't like the beautiful and strong men in the movies. He was just this kind, gentle man.

He kissed her again, then pulled back to look at her. And she looked at him, too. Openly. His smile, his kind eyes. And she let that thing inside herself, that kept-back place, that breath she'd held for as long as she could remember, release, expand.

He reached up and brushed back her hair again, followed the curve of her ear, drew his soft fingers along the rough of her jawline.

And she froze. It was like fog and a sick heat had come down on top of her.

Nothing had changed in his eyes. Nothing at all. She could see that. But his simple, loving touch had taken everything sweet and safe from the moment, had made her remember where she was, who she was. She pulled away.

"Thank you for the evening. I—I have to work the breakfast shift in the morning, so . . ." She stuck out her hand to him. My rough, ugly hand, she thought.

And now the light did change in Ben's eyes. Slowly, he took her hand in his and shook it.

"Of course. I'm so sorry; I didn't mean to keep you out so late. Good night, Miss Maureen."

And after she'd gone in, after she'd turned off the porch light, closed herself into her room, he sat there in the car, in the dark, for some time before he drove away.

THE MORNING WAS COOL and gray, it was her day off, and Maureen stayed in bed late.

She couldn't understand her own self, why she didn't just up and leave town right then. Because to live her life as she had to live it meant that she couldn't have the things that other women had. She'd never had a boyfriend, certainly not a lover. She didn't even really understand anything of romance and love, how it worked outside of seeing it in the movies. She knew it wasn't like that, not really. But what was it?

And then Ben Anders kissed her.

If she could ever let herself get close to anyone, it would be someone like him. Maybe they could still be friends. If that was all it was, if that's how they kept it, she could be happy, she thought. As long as he didn't want more, as long as he didn't try to make it something more than that.

But how do you stop something once it's started? How do you keep safe what you have so you don't lose it all? How can you make a person understand when you can't explain it to him, when you can't even explain it to yourself, when it's just how you are?

You don't understand, Ben, I just ain't like other women. Not like any other women.

By noon the sun had come out and Maureen went down to the bank and withdrew the fifty-seven dollars she had saved up there, then walked over to the bus depot and bought a ticket.

Late that afternoon, Mrs. Ralph knocked at the door. She had a letter.

In five years, Maureen had never had a letter.

After Mrs. Ralph handed it to her, turning back with a worried look on her face as she left the room, Maureen held the pale gray envelope pressed between her palms, turning one side up then the other, for a long time before she finally opened it.

"Dear Miss Maureen,

"I am very sorry if I offended you last night. I wouldn't want to do that for the world; you're such a fine person. I think you know that I hold you in the highest regard and, if I may say so, affection.

"If you do not feel toward myself anything of a romantic nature, I will completely respect your feelings, and we can say no more about that. I do not mean to cause embarrassment or to have created an awkward situation. My greatest hope is that, should this be the case, that you cannot return my feelings, we may still remain friends. We are two grown people, and sensible, and I think it possible. Do you agree?

"The only other thing, I just wanted to say that I think that there are all kinds of people in this world. I don't think it matters at all what kind of people a person is as long as they're a good person. And if some people are different than others—even so different it's hard to understand—as long as they don't hurt anybody, what does it matter? I don't know why I should need to say this to you, but I do.

"Again, I ask you to please forgive my impetuous behavior. If you do not choose to respond to this letter or to continue our acquaintance, I will surely understand.

"Yours respectfully,

"Ben Anders"

THAT NIGHT MAUREEN PULLED her old valise out from under the bed, opened it. She really hadn't much to put in it, not much more than what she came with; five years' worth of nothing. There was a bus to Phoenix in the morning.

After she'd taken down the scrap of fabric from the window, folded it, put it in the valise with her clothes and her movie magazines and the green satin pillow, she moved the chair to the middle of the room, got up onto it and reached for the paper lantern. So close to it as she untwisted the wires that held it in place, the pink and red light flowing over her upstretched arms, her upturned face, the shapes of roses dancing along her skin with each awkward movement against the light. Finally the lantern came free, exposing the bald glare of the bulb, and she squinted and turned away.

But Maureen stood there for a moment, on the chair, her hands folding down the volume of the lantern, collapsing it flat, the harsh weight of naked light along the broadness of her shoulders, catching the knobs of her wrist bones, the ridges of her knuckles, the strong bones of her brow, the glint of stubble along her jaw.

She stood there on that chair—exactly in the middle of the room, touching no wall, not the ceiling, not the floor—and remembered all the times she'd run before, the first time when she was only sixteen. The running away and the learning to survive and the struggle to pass. And the running again when that failed. But now, standing in this ugly light, this hard and truthful light, a light that Hollywood could never admit to, the thought of running away again, the worn-out safety of leaving and of loneliness, seemed more painful than any kind of hurt, harder than any kind of staying.

Maureen squinted up at the naked bulb so close above her head, felt the warmth of it on her face. Then she carefully unfolded the lantern—the fragile paper globe expanding, like taking in breath, each thin bamboo rib lifting away from each delicate rib—raised it above her head, gently wired it back into place—the light of red and pink roses flooding back into the room—and stepped down from the chair.

Afterword

I'VE NEVER BEEN what I'd consider a "serious" writer. I'm not in a writing group, I've never taken a writing workshop. I've only submitted work once or twice, only read in public a handful of times. I'm certainly not a disciplined writer. I've usually only been able to write a story—like the ones collected here—when that perverse, elusive thing called "inspiration" hits.

Even so, for my entire adult life, I've been making stories. The focus on my career as a painter and my public persona as such has, I think, discouraged me from pushing harder, from working more frequently at something I love but have feared wouldn't be taken seriously. Whether anyone else would think so, I still struggle with feeling like an imposter, almost an intruder, in this realm.

It's a strange thing to compare what I paint with what I write; the two are cast in sharply divergent tones. Of course it can be said that my paintings tell stories, too. Narratives that are usually light and precise, well-dressed and well-lit, elegant, often funny; the bright golden glow of each piece's underpainting is more than just a feature of this artist's technique.

The stories I write down come from some other place altogether, usually somewhere much darker. I create characters that are frequently placed—caught—in difficult, sometimes desperate, situations. People—old and young, of various genders and orientations—who are, through time and circumstance, faced with hard questions, people with serious choices that have to be made. I don't know why I put them there.

I've joked, while putting together this collection, calling this the most depressing little book ever. But, honestly, to me it isn't actually depressing. Because, as someone always searching out beauty, I recognize it in so many, often unexpected, forms. Because beauty isn't always pretty. Often it's sad and lost. That's what I find I'm compelled to write about, that's what is there inside me. I know that, just as in my paintings, I'm always trying to create something I can find beautiful. And I find beauty in both laughter and melancholy.

I understand that these stories are probably not what anyone would expect from me. They aren't necessarily what I'd expect from me. I can't begin to guess what anyone might think of the stories in this book, but they're true to what I intended them to be, true to some strata of my character that only appears in this form. As I've often said in regard to my painting, to explain my artistic inclinations, why I make what I make: Create the art you want to see in the world, satisfy your own very particular taste, without thought to any potential audience or critique, and the chances are good that someone, somewhere will find a connection with what you've made. I hope these stories might connect.

Acknowledgments

As TO HOW I got here:

To Steve Arndt, first of all.

To Tom Spanbauer and that table in the basement.

To all the Dangerous Writers, both table readers and "pond scum."

To Laura Stanfill and Forest Avenue Press.

To all the other publishers and writers that Gigi has worked with.

To Domi J. Shoemaker and the Burnt Tongue reading series.

To all the contributors to *The Untold Gaze*.

To the Henry writing group and The Gong Show writing group.

All of the above validated and encouraged Gigi's talent and drive as a writer and/or as a graphic designer, while I've never studied with or worked at writing with any of them. Listening to them read and discuss their work, though, I've been exposed to so much about the art and craft of writing. It's been so expanding, so inspiring, so instructive. Just being around them has taught me so much; I've always learned best by osmosis. Even more, I'm grateful for their friendship and that, right from the beginning, they welcomed me in, made me feel a part of this wonderful literary community even though, as far as they knew, I was—just—a painter.

I ALSO NEED TO EXPRESS my gratitude to those who first gave me a chance to share my work with the public:

To Shu-Ju Wang, and the reading series she included in her 2019 exhibition "Things That Don't Float."

To Elisa Saphier and her Another Read Through bookstore.

To Adam Strong and his Songbook PDX reading series.

And to Kirsten Larson who discovered and suggested "From the Streetcar" for inclusion in *Nailed Magazine*.

LASTLY, most importantly, I want to thank Gigi Little who, in addition to employing her well-known skills as a book designer/cover designer on this project, has been, all along, my one-person reading group, English teacher, and the most brilliant and tough and sensitive editor. If these stories succeed in any way, it is in huge part due to her patient and generous guidance.